She wound her arms swept her tongue inside his mouth, tasting tooth powder and inhaling his spicy cologne that reminded her of dark forests and misty mornings.

A groan rumbled up from his chest, striking an unexpected answering chord of pleasure deep within her body. She stroked her hands down his back while tasting and tangling her tongue with his. Delicious.

He lifted his head and gazed down at her. "Without question you entice me, Mrs. Durant. Do you mean to do so, I wonder?"

His directness made her smile. There was an honesty about him that was refreshing. He deserved an honest answer. After all, what was the point of beating around the bush at her time of life? "I most certainly do. Please call me Amelia."

He sucked in a breath, as if her words affected him physically. It seemed the attraction did indeed go both ways.

"Your reputation—"

"Is mine to care for, Your Grace."

He stroked a stray hair back from her face with a touch so light she scarcely felt it. "Jasper."

She smiled. "Jasper it is. In private, of course."

The heat in his gaze seemed to sear her face. "Well, Amelia, just how private are we?"

Author Note

It is always a surprise when I realize I have come to the end of the journey with my hero and heroine, and so it is with Jasper and Amelia. I very much enjoyed writing their story and I hope you enjoy reading it. I did quite a bit of digging around about the history of the Royal Observatory at Greenwich. What a fascinating subject. I love that I can delve into a bit of history during the course of writing my story and I hope you enjoy it, too. I love to hear from readers; you can always reach me through my website at annlethbridge.com.

ANN LETHBRIDGE

The Matchmaker
and the Duke

HARLEQUIN®
HISTORICAL™

Recycling programs
for this product may
not exist in your area.

ISBN-13: 978-1-335-50540-8

The Matchmaker and the Duke

Copyright © 2020 by Michéle Ann Young

All rights reserved. No part of this book may be used or reproduced in
any manner whatsoever without written permission except in the case of
brief quotations embodied in critical articles and reviews.

This is a work of fiction. Names, characters, places and incidents
are either the product of the author's imagination or are used fictitiously.
Any resemblance to actual persons, living or dead, businesses,
companies, events or locales is entirely coincidental.

This edition published by arrangement with Harlequin Books S.A.

For questions and comments about the quality of this book,
please contact us at CustomerService@Harlequin.com.

Harlequin Enterprises ULC
22 Adelaide St. West, 40th Floor
Toronto, Ontario M5H 4E3, Canada
www.Harlequin.com

Printed in U.S.A.

In her youth, award-winning author **Ann Lethbridge** reimagined the Regency romances she read—and now she loves writing her own. Now living in Canada, Ann visits Britain every year, where family members understand—or so they say—her need to poke around every antiquity within a hundred miles. Learn more about Ann or contact her at annlethbridge.com. She loves hearing from readers.

Books by Ann Lethbridge

Harlequin Historical

It Happened One Christmas
"Wallflower, Widow...Wife!"
Secrets of the Marriage Bed
Rescued by the Earl's Vows
The Matchmaker and the Duke

The Widows of Westram

A Lord for the Wallflower Widow
An Earl for the Shy Widow
A Family for the Widowed Governess

The Society of Wicked Gentlemen

An Innocent Maid for the Duke

Visit the Author Profile page
at Harlequin.com for more titles.

This book is dedicated to Joanne Grant, my very first editor at Harlequin. I would not be where I am today with my writing without her patience, perseverance and excellent advice.

Chapter One

1817

'Jasper, it is high time you married.'

Jasper Simon Warren, Duke of Stone, Marquess of Felmont and Earl Blackmore, despised conversation at breakfast. He did not raise his gaze from his newspaper. 'I see.'

'Jasper, did you hear what I said? You have a duty to the dukedom.'

The sharp edge in her voice indicated Aunt Mary was not going to take the hint.

He lowered his newspaper a fraction. 'Are you accusing me of neglecting my duties, Aunt?' He let the ice in his tone sink into her awareness.

The spring sun, streaming through the windows of the ducal town house, gave no quarter to the elderly lady. Dressed in a forest-green gown and lace cap of the latest fashion, the wrinkles in her cheeks and around her mouth, the thinness of her carefully primped hair, proclaimed a woman well past her sixtieth year. 'Certainly not, Jasper. I simply want you to be happy.'

He stared at her in astonishment. 'I assure you, I am perfectly content.'

The creases in her forehead deepened. 'Contentment is not the same as happiness.'

'Who defines happiness? And since when has society latched upon the idea that happiness is vital to a person's existence?'

After years of observing the marriages of his peers from the sidelines, he had few illusions.

And yet... 'My parents were happy, were they not?'

'I never heard anything to the contrary.'

Hardly a ringing endorsement. Had he perhaps imagined them as happy? Created a fantasy to ease the loss? Was he wrong to aspire to the sort of joy he recalled in their presence? And could he have been mistaken about the truth of it?

Aunt Mary made a sound of impatience. 'Besides, no matter what, the dukedom needs an heir.'

The real reason for her fussing. 'All in good time.' He raised his paper, focusing on the article on the latest arguments for Parliamentary reform.

'You are not getting any younger,' she muttered.

Really! He folded his newspaper and put it down beside his plate where a few crumbs of toast and a smear of marmalade were all that remained of what *had* been a very fine breakfast. 'I am thirty-five. Not exactly in my dotage.'

'You will be thirty-six next month. I want to see things settled before I go to my final rest.'

His jaw dropped. 'Are you ill? Shall I send for a physician?'

She coloured high on her cheekbones. 'Certainly not. But, Jasper, time is running out. The Season is well underway and those looking for wives will snap up the most eligible girls in a trice.'

He raised an eyebrow. 'Are you suggesting that should I indicate an interest in a female, she will turn me down for someone she met earlier in the Season?'

'Of course not. No woman in their right mind would turn down an offer from the Duke of Stone.'

Even if they wanted to, as he had learned in his youth. He pushed the unpleasant memory aside. Dwelling on the past helped no one. 'Well, my dear Aunt Mary, since I have no intention of offering for a woman who is not in her right mind, I can see no reason for haste.' He eyed his newspaper. He would take it to his study. No one would dare interrupt him there.

'They would refuse you if they had already accepted another offer. How do you know there is not a lady among this latest group to come out whom you would not prefer above all others?'

'I am sure all of them are respectable young women whose parents would leap at a crown of strawberry leaves. I do not expect to encounter any difficulties.'

'How can you know, Stone, if you do not look?' Her voice was full of exasperation. She shook her head. 'There is no point in talking to you about this, I can see. But take my advice, marry now while you are still in your prime. No one knows what the future holds.'

He frowned. Aunt Mary was making more of a fuss about this than she had about anything since… since he could not remember when. And, yes, he knew he had to bestir himself at some point. Find the right sort of woman to be his Duchess. He simply had not thought of it as urgent. Nor was it. Yet his aunt seemed genuinely distressed. 'Very well. To please you, I will take a look at this year's crop.'

A veritable study of nonchalance, she picked up a pile of invitations set by her plate and sorted through them. She didn't fool him for a moment.

'Was there something you wanted to add?'

She put the cards down with a snap. 'There are two girls whom you might wish to meet. The Mitchell sisters. Both outrageously lovely, reasonably well bred and exceedingly well dowered. I saw them at Lady Dobson's musical evening last night.'

'Lady Dobson?' A chill invaded his veins. 'Not exactly the cream of the *ton*, my dear. Not the sort of company I like to keep. And I assume by reasonably well bred you mean not of the peerage?'

His aunt grimaced. 'Sally Jersey suggested I attend to take a look at them. She'd heard much about their beauty and accomplishments and requested my opinion. Both presented exceedingly well. Another pair like the Gunning girls, I would say.'

The Gunning sisters were still talked about in the drawing rooms of the *ton*. They had taken London by storm and married well above their station. 'Not the sort of wife *I* seek.'

'Then you are looking.' She sounded so relieved, he did not have the heart to disabuse her of the notion. Aunt Mary was one of the few people whose feelings he cared about. Not that she usually got up in the boughs about anything. She certainly must be feeling her age if she was panicking about marrying him off. And she wasn't entirely wrong to be concerned. It was time.

He sighed. 'Do not expect me to attend events hosted by the likes of Lady Dobson.' Her husband, a banker, had been knighted by the King for services rendered. Likely a personal loan or an inside tip on a profitable investment. Not a member of the nobility.

'Certainly not. You know better than to ask. Mrs Durant has them in hand. After my endorsement you will meet them at all the best parties.'

'Durant?'

'Three years ago, her husband broke his neck in a steeplechase.'

Ah, yes. 'I remember him. A reckless idiot. I do not recall a wife.'

'She was a Linden. Her cousin holds the viscountcy now. She has become well known for her matchmaking skills.'

'You seriously think I should consider one of these girls?' It sounded so unlike his aunt, he could not keep the curiosity out of his voice.

'I have been throwing eminently eligible daughters of the *ton* in your path for the past ten years and not once have you shown any interest. I thought perhaps your taste was so jaded, I should try something different.'

Jaded? He wasn't jaded. Cynical. There was a description he could own, too. He'd had enough toadies and sycophants trying to get his attention since he inherited the title at the age of fifteen that he could spot one a mile off. But he wasn't jaded. He was comfortable. He had a small group of friends, mostly male, whose wealth meant they did not seek to use him for their own ends and therefore whom he trusted.

He also had a mistress, Jane Garnet, whose favours he had enjoyed to the full for many years. A woman with whom he had agreed upon an exclusive arrangement, who was quite content to entertain him whenever he felt the need.

'I suppose next you will be telling me I should pay off Mrs Garnet.'

His aunt rifled through the invitations and did not meet his gaze. 'It might be as well.'

Damn it all.

It seemed his life of comfort was slipping away.

'I thought the older girl might be ideal for you. And the younger for Albert.'

She spoke this last in such a low tone, he almost missed it. Aunt Mary continually thought to push Albert Carling, the only surviving relative on her mother's side, up society's ladder. Marriage to an heiress would certainly gild his path.

At one time, Jasper had been close with Albert.

Unfortunately, Albert had not proved true and now they remained cordial but distant.

Three ladies tried to ignore Mr Mitchell pacing the drawing room of the town house he had rented close to Bedford Square. Two were his daughters, Charity and Patience, both blonde, pretty and making their come out in the London Season. The other, Mrs Amelia Durant, a lady with dark hair and eyes, was approaching her thirtieth year. While she was sure that she herself had never been deemed a great beauty, she had been born into the highest of society's circles and she wearied of Mr Mitchell and his tirades.

'Mrs Durant, I was told you know all the best people and can find the right husbands for my daughters.' He paused and stared over his pince-nez at Amelia on the morning after his daughters' first foray into the *ton*. 'Now you tell me there wasn't a single earl or duke at that party.'

'Oh, Papa,' Charity Mitchell said, raising her blue eyes from her needlework to meet his stern gaze. She gave him a sweet smile. 'Lord Philpot was there and Sir Robert…something. I forget.' She glanced over at Amelia.

'Lord Robert Partere,' she supplied. 'A very old family with excellent connections.'

Amelia had explained her plan to Mr Mitchell more than once, but he didn't seem to grasp the need for a light touch. Marrying girls off to suitable gentlemen, especially those of the nobility, was a very delicate matter. The girls might be utterly lovely, but their background was strictly middle class.

She repressed a sigh of exasperation. 'Last night was not about seeking suitors—'

'Then what was it about?' he grumbled.

'It was about assuring the *ton* that your lovely daughters can safely be invited to the most exclusive of parties and behave like proper young ladies.' She beamed at the girls. 'And they both passed muster, I can assure you. Lady Mary Warren was most complimentary about their looks and demeanour.'

It had taken Amelia nigh on three months to ensure that the girls knew exactly how to behave in polite company and to eliminate any trace of the broad Yorkshire vowels that coloured their papa's conversation.

The *ton* would not care about the merchant father, as long as he settled a suitable amount on his beautiful daughters and stayed clear of their new families. On the other hand, the daughters must be untainted by their humble origins if they were to attract an offer from the most eligible of bachelors.

Amelia knew exactly how to ensure such young ladies met suitable and honourable gentlemen. Honourable being the key word. She had been doing it for years. The *ton* trusted her to endorse only the sweetest and most rigorously trained young women to the scions of the nobility. The parents of those hopeful young people quickly learned to follow her directions to the letter if they wanted to utilise her services, for which she was paid handsomely. Her fees were based on the settlements negotiated between the parties once the marriages were arranged.

The Mitchell sisters were proving to be more of a challenge than any before them. True, their undeniable beauty made them viable prospects and their amiable natures had made her like them from their first meeting. So much so, she had willingly taken them under her wing.

Unfortunately, their widowed papa, a man who had pulled himself up by his bootstraps, as he was proud to tell all and sundry, was irascible and inclined to want to rush things. He did not value her counsel as he ought and the lack of a wife to make him see reason was a drawback. Mind you, it would have to be a pretty strong woman to stand up to Papa Mitchell. His daughters certainly were not up to the task. Amelia was beginning to think she had not made a wise decision in offering to assist them in their search for husbands among the nobility.

'Who is Lady Mary Warren, when she is at home?' Mr Mitchell asked, folding his arms across his chest. He was a portly man with a round florid face and his once blond hair was now mostly grey and thinning on top. 'I have never heard of her.'

'Papa,' Patience Mitchell said, pressing her hands together. 'You really should have paid more attention to Mrs Durant's lessons from *Debrett's Peerage*. She is the aunt of the wealthiest Duke in all of Britain.'

'And he is the youngest,' Charity said. She frowned. 'Though he is thirty-five.'

'A man in his prime, then,' their father said.

Both girls looked uncertain. 'Thirty-five seems awfully old,' Charity said. She looked at Amelia for confirmation.

'Thirty-five is not terribly old,' Amelia said. If it was then she would be terribly old in five years' time. 'But the Duke of Stone has been on the town for years and has shown no interest in settling down. Honestly, he is not a man I would recommend setting your cap at. The Duke is very high in the instep. He is unlikely to make an offer for anyone below the daughter of an earl.'

'You sound as if you do not like him,' Patience said.

Patience was both the younger of the sisters and, in Amelia's estimation, the brighter. Their papa seemed to favour his older daughter Charity. But there really wasn't much to choose between them. Like most young ladies in their first Season their heads were stuffed full of romantic notions. Amelia's had certainly been, which was why it had been so easy for Lieutenant Durant to sweep her off her feet. He'd been every young lady's vision of a knight in shining armour. Amelia no longer believed such men existed. Or if they did, then they certainly did not make very good husbands.

'I was introduced to him,' she said, recalling that day as if it was yesterday, 'I truly cannot say I know him, except by reputation.' And by observation over the years. The man was insufferably proud, though always exceedingly polite. He struck her as a man without any great feelings or emotions.

Yes, she had felt a spark of attraction at their first meeting, but it had been quickly extinguished when a few days later his gaze passed over her as if she had never crossed his path. Clearly, he did not care to remember any of lesser mortals who floated through his orbit.

It wasn't long after her encounter with him that she had met and married Tarquin Durant. Widowed two years' later, she had returned to London to set up her own modest establishment and found herself helping a cousin avoid a marital disaster by uncovering the prospective bridegroom's shady past.

Not only that, she had guided the young woman to catch the most eligible bachelor of the Season, or at least the second most eligible. Stone was always the first. From there, she had built a reputation as a matchmaker *par excellence*. The money she had earned these past three years had provided her with a decent life, a small town house of her own in a select neighbourhood and she was able to help young people enter into good sensible marriages. Something she had failed to do.

'Are you saying you think my girls are beneath him?' Papa Mitchell said, glaring.

'Certainly not.' Amelia smiled calmly. 'Your daughters will be a credit to any gentleman. But the Duke is very conscious of his family pedigree.'

The belligerence in Mr Mitchell increased tenfold. 'Then I say he is not good enough for my daughters.'

Amelia closed her eyes briefly. 'Let us not focus on Stone. Let us turn our attention to the bachelors whom we will meet over the next few weeks and who will make fine husbands for your daughters.'

'Titled gentlemen,' Mitchell snapped.

'Young gentlemen with good prospects and honourable intentions who will make excellent husbands. I do not promise a title, but any gentleman I recommend will be acceptable on every ground.'

'One of the Gunning sisters married a duke and the other an earl,' Patience said.

'One of them married two dukes,' Charity added.

The girls burst into giggles. They looked so merry and so pretty, Amelia let their amusement pass without comment. However, she would caution them not to model themselves on the Gunning sisters. Yes, they had both married well, but they had also been embroiled in scandal.

The *ton* turned a blind eye to a certain amount of indiscretion from among their own, but not from outsiders like the Mitchell girls. If their papa continued to reject her advice, her reputation for bringing only the most suitable young ladies to the notice of the upper one thousand could be tarnished. She might be forced to terminate their agreement.

As Jasper had expected, Lady Jersey's ball could only be described as a squeeze. But then it would be. The Countess of Jersey was one of the patronesses of Almack's and not one to be lightly snubbed. By the time Jasper arrived, guests already blocked the stairs up to the first-floor drawing room while they awaited their turn to be announced. With an impatient sigh, he did what he usually did upon these occasions, he headed for the green-baize-covered door tucked discreetly beneath the impressive staircase and, with a nod and a coin slipped into a waiting palm, ascended by way of the servants' stairs.

Why on earth people felt the need to have their names blared into a room full of chattering guests he would never understand. No one inside was listening apart from the host and hostess. Besides, everyone knew everyone else anyway. And if they didn't, they probably were not worth knowing.

He glanced around the crowded ballroom, seeking a friendly face. His hostess spotted him and immediately left the line at the door to greet him. 'Up to your usual tricks, Duke?' she said with a smile.

She'd caught him entering this way when he was much younger and had teased him about it ever since. He continued the practice almost as a point of honour. Well, that and the fact that it saved him from having long arduous conversations with people who saw it as an opportunity to curry his favour on some matter or other.

'What else can I do when you insist upon inviting every member of the *ton* to your balls, Sally?'

She made a face. 'I hate anyone to be disappointed.'

It was why she handed out tickets for Almack's in such a free-handed way. She was the despair of the other patronesses.

'You are too soft-hearted.'

'Whereas you are as cold as stone.'

He grinned, enjoying that she said exactly what popped into her head instead of beating around the bush as so many ladies did when they spoke to him. 'And here I thought no one had guessed.'

She shook her head at him. 'One of these days you will get your comeuppance, Duke. Mark my words.'

He bowed and moved on. He joined a group of gentlemen at the end of the room furthest from the orchestra. Men he'd known for years, some from his university days, others from his first Season. Most were now married with children and were in town to take their seats in the House of Lords. Parliament was the reason the nobility came to London for the Season. Somehow, the ladies had turned it into a marriage mart.

Jasper looked about him.

The ball was the same as every other event he had attended. The latest crop of debutantes stood in little clumps around the edge of the dance floor, trying to look as if they didn't care that no one had asked them to dance and failing miserably. The diamonds of the first water smiled happily as they proved their superiority on the dance floor and the matrons gossiped while they kept an eye on their daughters. Meanwhile, the wallflowers, those gals who had been out a Season or three, lurked in the corners as if they had lost all hope.

Now he remembered why he preferred his club to a night of dancing.

It was not long before Sally sought him out once

more. 'It is time you met the Mitchell sisters. Let me make the introductions.'

Jasper did not like the feeling of being swept along willy-nilly and almost refused. But dash it, his curiosity was aroused. Sally guided him towards a large group of people gathered near the orchestra. At the centre of the cluster of young ladies and gentlemen were two blonde girls with shining blue eyes and curvaceous figures, dressed in white, tastefully modest gowns.

To Jasper's surprise, Sally did not make a beeline for these two lovelies, but to the woman hovering near them. A woman certainly past the first blush of youth, but who was quite exotically beautiful with dark hair and dark eyes, and skin that hinted of warmer climes than chilly England. His heart seemed to miss a beat. It was as if his recognition of her beauty had interrupted its rhythm. A most unpleasant sensation. And why on earth did he have the feeling he had met her before?

'Mrs Durant, may I introduce to you the Duke of Stone,' Sally said.

Ah, yes, Mrs Durant, the matchmaker Aunt Mary had mentioned. He had not expected her to be such a beauty, given her line of work. And there was that odd sensation that he had met her somewhere before.

The woman's eyes widened a fraction as her gaze met his. Her irises were the colour of toffee with a starburst of gold in their centres.

Beautiful eyes, with unexpected warmth. He knew those eyes. The colours changed, darkened.

'I believe we are old acquaintances,' he said. If only he could recall the occasion of their meeting.

A flash of surprise crossed her face, quickly replaced by a cool smile. 'How kind of you to remember, Your Grace.'

Devil take it, he prided himself on never forgetting a face. It had taken him years to hone the skill, but it stood him in good stead when dealing with the myriad of people for whom he was responsible in some way. Then why was he having troubling recalling *where* he had met her? And when? And why did he have the odd feeling she did not like him? Had he given offence in some way? He bowed. 'My pleasure.'

'Let me introduce you to my charges.' The briskness of her words took him aback. She definitely did not like him.

'It seems you are in good hands, Duke,' Sally said. 'I will leave you to Mrs Durant's good graces.' She sailed off as swiftly as she had arrived. The woman could not be still for a moment.

Turning towards the blonde girls, Mrs Durant presented him with a startlingly striking profile. A sculptor would have had difficulty imagining such a combination of strong yet purely feminine features. They were features that might give a man endless hours of fascinating exploration. And her skin, so warm in colour, so delicately smooth—he found himself wanting to stroke a finger along her angular jaw to see if it was as silky as it appeared.

He forced his gaze to the two young ladies looking at him expectantly. Yes, they were young and very

pretty, but beside their chaperon they paled into in-
significance. At least in his opinion.

'Your Grace,' Mrs Durant said with a measure
of pride, 'may I present, Miss Charity Mitchell and
her sister, Miss Patience. Ladies, the Duke of Stone.'

Both girls curtsied and showed their dimples.

He bowed. 'How are you enjoying your first Season, ladies?' he asked.

It was a trite question, but it had served him in
good stead over the years.

'We are having a grand time,' the younger, Miss
Patience, said.

'This is only our second ball,' Miss Mitchell
added. 'I do not think I have seen so many people
in a ballroom. I had no idea people had ballrooms of
this size in their houses.'

Their honesty and frank way of speaking surprised
him. It was refreshing. They spoke like normal people
instead of giggling twits.

He glanced back at their chaperon. Mrs Durant
seemed to be eyeing him warily as if she suspected
his motives for seeking an introduction. He racked
his brains for some misdemeanour in his past that
would account for her attitude.

Or was she simply assessing him as a likely suitor?
The idea she would presume that she could choose a
wife for him appalled him. Though it did not surprise
him one whit. As soon as people heard his title, they
sought a way to use him to further their own ends.
Why would she be any different? To be sure, the girls
were tricked out as fine as five pence and looked as

pretty as pictures, but they did not hale from the nobility. It was from those ranks he had always expected he would select a bride.

Mrs Durant lifted her chin in challenge, as if reading his thoughts. Why on earth had he thought her beautiful? Her features were arresting, yes, but they gave her face and expression strength, not beauty.

Unfortunately, since he had sought an introduction, if he did not do his duty and ask one of them to dance, the *ton* might well see it as a mark of his displeasure, when he really felt nothing at all.

He smiled briefly at the older of the two. 'Will you do the honour of joining me in the fourth set of the evening, Miss Mitchell?'

The girl blushed and glanced at her chaperon, who nodded. She bobbed a curtsy. 'Thank you, Your Grace.'

He bowed. 'I will return for you then.'

As he strolled away, whispers and giggles broke out behind him as everyone realised that the Duke of Stone had actually unbent enough to invite the latest diamond of the first water to dance.

Would Mrs Durant see it as a feather in her cap?

Chapter Two

Amelia could not understand Stone's game. Was he actually looking for a bride? Lady Warren had not given a hint of any such thing when she had spoken to Amelia, but it might account for her friendliness at the Dobsons' musicale.

If he was finally considering doing his duty to the title, it would account for his unbending enough to actually seek an introduction to the girls. Hopefully it was a passing fancy on his part. Charity and Patience were nice young women and deserved better than a man whose consequence led him to look down on the rest of the world. Handsome he might be, but he was as cold as his name.

She let go a breath. Perhaps she was being unfair, letting her prejudice against him colour her judgement of his character. Certainly, if Stone was pleased enough to offer to dance with Charity, then the Mitchell girls would instantly be accepted into the arms of the *ton* with no help from Amelia.

For some reason, his power to approved or disapprove annoyed her more than anything.

One thing Amelia did know for certain, Stone was not in need of a wealthy wife. Therefore, the idea that he would select a girl who was so far beneath him, as these two were, boggled her mind. Unless he was smitten.

Her heart twisted. Worry for the girls, that was all it was. Because she certainly had seen no sign of any such thing in Stone's demeanour towards Charity. He had been as haughty and reserved as she remembered.

Good lord! Surely he did not have dishonourable intentions? If so, she would have to make it very clear he was completely out of line. She narrowed her gaze on the broad shoulders easing their way through the milling crowds. He was clearly a man who took regular exercise. He had not run to seed as so many did when approaching middle age. He was more physically impressive now than he had been when she first met him.

Charity touched her arm, clearly dying to ask a question. Amelia allowed a few moments to elapse before discreetly drawing her a little apart from the group. 'Is everything all right?'

'Not really. I wanted to dance the fourth set with Lord Sherbourn, not the Duke. I was too afraid to refuse him.'

Stone was enough to intimidate the hardiest females and refusing him might well have been a disaster for Charity and her sister.

Amelia took a steadying breath. Even if Stone was

not a serious suitor, he could not be taken lightly. 'I could tell you were nervous from the way you were chattering. Try to take a deep breath before you speak, it will let your brain catch up to your tongue.' She gave the girl an encouraging smile. 'But you did very well, my dear. The Duke must have been pleased with you or he would not have asked you to stand up with him. Had you already told Lord Sherbourn you would stand up with him for that set?'

'No. I could see he was plucking up the courage to ask me and I was doing everything I could to encourage him and then the Duke came along.'

'Well, there are lots more dances this evening. Encourage him to ask for one of those.'

The girl nodded and looked more cheerful. 'I will.' She rejoined her friends with a bright smile.

A friend of Lady Dobson's son from university, Sherbourn had also been at the Dobsons' musical evening. Amelia knew his family sought a wife with money for him. A good settlement would solve their most pressing problems after a bad marine investment had battered the family's finances.

Amelia had investigated the Sherbourns thoroughly and, until this loss, they had proven to be of solid worth. Not a scrap of scandal or irresponsibility marred their reputation. In addition, as well as heir to a title, Sherbourn was a pleasant-spoken, nice-looking young man, if a little too passionate about things.

Nothing like the Duke of Stone.

A middle-aged woman in grey silk sailed up to Amelia, fanning her full round red face. 'Now that would be a feather in your cap.' Lady Dobson looked a little miffed.

Amelia smiled politely. 'I beg your pardon?'

'The Duke. Making sheep's eyes at the older Mitchell sister.'

Amelia kept her expression coolly polite. 'Do you think so?'

Lady Dobson wanted either of the Mitchell girls for her own son, Harold, a rather studious and inarticulate young man who actually didn't need to marry for wealth. Unfortunately, the poor young man was so weedy and his face so spotty, he was unlikely to attract any girl's attention without a great deal of help.

'I would not trust him to make either of them a proposal,' Lady Dobson said.

Amelia bridled. Why that would be, given she had been thinking something very similar a few moments before, she did not know. 'I have never heard it said that the Duke was anything but the most honourable of men.' Good heavens, was she defending him?

Lady Dobson's gaze fell away. 'You can't tell me he would choose beauty over position.'

No. That she could not. But he might choose wealth.

'They are such lovely girls, a man would have to be blind not to want to meet them,' Amelia said, trying to sort through her impressions of the Duke in her own mind. 'Likely he heard the gossip and came to see for himself. A man of the Duke's address would not dream of being introduced to a lady and not asking her to dance.' A feeling of relief went through her.

Of course, that was his reason. Thank goodness, despite his haughty attitude, he was indeed a gentleman.

Years ago, when Amelia had been introduced to him, he had not asked her to dance. Indeed, he'd barely said a word and had looked down his nose at the daughter of a mere baronet. She, on the other hand, had stared at his handsome face in awe and blushed furiously.

The besotted look on her face must have been pitiable. When she'd attempted to speak to him the next time they met, his blank look had left her wishing the floor would open.

Lady Dobson gave her a kindly smile. 'Well, if I were you, I would warn Miss Mitchell not to set her heart on him. I have heard it said he will not consider anyone below the daughter of an earl.'

She wasn't some green girl that needed that sort of advice. 'Would Harold like to dance with Patience?' Oddly enough, Patience had indicated that she quite liked the spotty young gentleman.

Lady Dobson brightened. 'He would love to dance with Miss Patience.'

'She has the third set available, if he is not otherwise engaged.' Patience had asked Amelia to relay this information to Mr Dobson, in case he did not get around to asking himself.

Lady Dobson bustled off.

While Mr Mitchell might have set his sights higher for his daughter, Patience and Mr Dobson liked each other a great deal. Amelia promised only to bring young people together whom she thought would suit. Couples she thought fit well together.

She glanced over to where Stone was engaged in deep conversation with Lord Jersey. Stone would certainly meet Papa Mitchell's expectation. Not to mention it would be a feather in Amelia's cap to marry one of her girls off to a duke. But she honestly could not see him as a suitable husband for either girl, if she wanted them to be happy.

And that *was* a primary consideration, no matter what their father thought.

Dancing with Miss Mitchell proved to be mildly entertaining in spite of Jasper's reservations. Her artless comments and her bright smile were refreshing. To boot, not once had she simpered or batted her eyelashes. While her parentage was unashamedly middle class, a few discreet enquiries had informed him that her father was well respected in the business community as a man as honest and hardworking as the day was long. The sort of man Jasper respected.

The sort of man upon whom England's future would be built. Those in Parliament needed to recognise this if they did not want to go the way of the French aristocracy. They needed to make it easier for men like Mitchell to achieve their goals, because the land alone could no longer support England's growing population. A population that wanted to have a say in their future.

On the other hand, he, as Duke, had also to think of his family's future. His bride ought to bring more

with her than wealth. Influence was far more important these days. In his opinion, the only way to bring
England into the future without destroying it was to
loosen the reins of power without giving them up entirely. Bring men like Mitchell into the fold, as it were.

He glanced over at the matchmaker, Mrs. Durant.
Did she understand that and was she congratulating
herself right now on having snagged the biggest marital coup of the decade? It was early days yet. While
he could see the benefits of marrying out of the nobility, he would have to live with the woman for the
rest of his life. His stomach dipped.

Perhaps he'd feel better about it if he took the time
to get to know Miss Mitchell. On the other hand, if
he let the grass grow under his feet, the matchmaker
would have no difficulty placing these girls now he
had given his stamp of approval by dancing with one
of them. And she was pleasant and exceedingly sweet.

And yet he felt a sense of something missing. He
had felt nothing but a sort of avuncular kindness for
the girl. Perhaps he really was getting old.

Devil take it. All that blathering by Aunt Mary
about happiness had somehow wormed its way into
his mind. He was perfectly happy…content…or something. He certainly did not enjoy being around people
in the throes of passion. It made him uncomfortable.

A pang twisted painfully in his chest as he recalled his parents' loving relationship. At one time
he had dreamed of something similar. But perhaps
it had been a child's illusion. He'd certainly not seen

that happiness in many of the marriages around him in the *ton*. He deliberately pushed the memory aside.

Fortunately, the figures of the dance left him and Miss Mitchell standing out at the top of the set. He focused his attention on her and she beamed at him.

'I suppose all of this must seem like old hat to you?' she said. 'At your time of life, you must have been to a great many balls and parties.'

His time of life? Good Lord, now he sounded as old as Methuselah. Challenged by the implication, he gave her his most charming of smiles. 'I have attended a great many balls, Miss Mitchell. But you know,' he said, leaning closer, 'it is the people who make them interesting.'

Her eyes widened a fraction, her lips parted. 'How—how do you mean?'

Yes, he had not completely lost his touch. He could still charm a young lady if he put his mind to it.

'For example, take the young gentleman over there with his mother, the plump dark-haired lady in the rose silk gown. That is Lord Barnaby. You would not think to look at him that he has devoted all of his time to working on a new sort of engine. If it works, it will make bringing goods to London much faster than ever before.'

She wrinkled her little nose. 'Why would speed be important?'

'Well… Say you want to sell fish caught in the rivers in Scotland. Right now, it comes to London by ship, but storms can delay that ship for days, even weeks. If it came by land in half the time it takes by boat, it would be fresher and command a better price.'

'Ew! I do not like fish.'

He laughed at the face of distaste she made. 'You might like it better if it was fresh.'

She shook her head. 'No, I know I would not. I have eaten it fresh from the river, but I do take your meaning, I suppose.'

'There are many other things that would also benefit from faster travel. I am sure you can think of some.'

She looked thoughtful for a moment. 'Oh, yes. Milk. Cream. Strawberries.'

Yes, she did understand. He smiled at her as they began their promenade down the dance. He had not expected to enjoy conversing with the young lady, but it made such a refreshing change, he was actually enjoying himself.

'How long have you been in London?' he asked.

'Almost six weeks.'

'You came right at the beginning of the Season, then.'

'Mrs Durant insisted we do so. She has been teaching us a great deal about how to go on, now and in the future.'

Ah yes, Mrs Durant. He glanced over to where the matchmaker was standing with a couple of older women. He could not help once more wondering what it was that he had done to make her dislike him.

'Is she very strict in her notions?' he asked.

'Not really. She mostly tells us to be ourselves,

but not to giggle or be silly. She also had us take elocution lessons to make us speak more clearly and dancing lessons to make sure we know all the latest steps and music.'

A sensible woman, Mrs Durant, apparently. Giggling females were deucedly annoying and a young lady who could not dance was a liability. The dance parted them and they travelled individually up the behind the line of dancers in their set. They met again at the top, but they were not standing out, so there was no real opportunity to continue their conversation.

He moved through the figures of the dance intuitively. Did Mrs Durant know how to dance? He would like to see that lithe figure of hers on the dance floor. Especially in a waltz. She had the elegance to carry it off to perfection. He could also guess how well her body would move beneath his hands in other circumstances. His blood heated.

He stilled. What the devil was he doing? Dancing with one woman and thinking about another and in the most licentious of ways. It was not like him at all.

He forced himself to concentrate on the dance and his partner until the music came to an end and he escorted her to her chaperon. Mrs Durant smiled at Miss Mitchell. 'Here is Sir Robert come to claim his dance,' she said as a young gentleman approached.

The two greeted each other like old friends and joined a set on the far side of the dance floor where he could see the other sister standing up with a skinny young man.

'Your charges do you proud, Mrs Durant,' he said.

She looked startled. Whether it was what he had said or that he had spoken, he wasn't sure.

She inclined her head. 'Thank you, Your Grace.'

'Will you honour me with this next dance?'

This time her jaw dropped. 'Me? You are asking me to dance?'

He bowed, slightly. 'I spoke in English and I believe my meaning is clear.'

She choked back a laugh and for a moment he thought she might say yes. He waited for her acceptance with a feeling of anticipation.

'Goodness me, no,' she said, the gold in her eyes twinkling as if she thought he had been merely teasing. A faint trace of colour appeared high on her cheekbones. 'I do not dance.'

Along with surprise that any woman would turn him down, an unexpected sense of disappointment filled him. He bowed and it felt a little stiff, even as he retained a pleasant smile. 'Then if you will excuse me, I see a lady against the wall who might care to join me.'

After all, he could not dance with only one lady this evening. That would be tantamount to an offer of marriage. No doubt, one mistake and he'd find himself leg-shackled if Mrs Durant had anything to say about it. Resentment filled him.

Whether it was the thought of being trapped into marriage or because she had refused to dance, he could not decide.

In Amelia's opinion, Mr Mitchell had been lucky to rent such suitable lodgings, so close to Mayfair.

Located on a street off Bedford Square, it was a little cramped and the girls had to share a bedroom, but it was an address that would not be looked down upon by members of the *ton*. Indeed, they had some of those same members as neighbours.

The two girls, now in their nightgowns, sprawled on Charity's bed with their nightly hot chocolate. They made such a pretty picture together. Amelia sat in the rocking chair beside the hearth, sipping a cup of tea.

'Well?' Charity asked once the maid had finished tidying up and left. 'What do you think?'

Each evening they spent a half-hour or so reviewing the day's events and planning the next day before Amelia went home in the Mitchells' carriage.

Amelia stared into her tea. What she thought was not a subject for discussion with the girls. No, indeed. And yet she could not stop thinking about the smile in His Grace's eyes when he had asked her to dance. What on earth had he been thinking? Was it some sort of nasty jest? And yet...

She pushed the thought aside and smiled calmly. 'I think you girls were a credit to your papa this evening.'

Both girls beamed with delight.

'And a credit to you,' Charity said. 'I hope?'

'Oh, indeed. Very much so,' Amelia replied. 'I could not have been more pleased.'

'I was never more nervous that when I was dancing with the Duke,' Charity said. She giggled. 'He is so…so old and, I don't know, distant, even while being exceedingly polite. And…quite kind.'

A little pain stabbed Amelia in the region of her heart. If only he had been kind to her all those years ago, she might not have rushed into Durant's arms. But then she had never been as beautiful as Charity or Patience. Indeed, she had always felt like a bit of an ugly duckling during her come out and had been thrilled at Durant's attention. More fool she. Well, she had learned her lesson and whatever the Duke's motive for asking her to stand up with him tonight, she had scotched it nicely. If only she didn't feel…sad.

'Do you think he will make Charity an offer?' Patience asked and giggled.

Charity looked horrified. 'Oh, no. He won't. Will he? Good gracious me, I do hope not.'

Amelia felt a stab of irritation. 'Even if he does not, what the Duke did by dancing with you was establish you as a girl of acceptable quality in the eyes of the *ton*.'

Both girls stared at her open-mouthed.

Amelia winced. Perhaps she had been a little too forceful. 'And one dance does not mean a betrothal is in the offing. However, he is a leader in society. If he approves, so will every other member of his set.' She inhaled a little breath, trying to maintain her aura of calm. 'And by only dancing with you once and asking three other debutantes to dance, he put you firmly in the same echelon as the daughters of earls and viscounts.'

Charity nodded wisely. 'Then I must be grateful to him, I suppose.'

Amelia smiled. 'Be yourself, Charity. That is what pleased him in the first place, I am sure.'

'But you don't think he is…courting me?'

Her stomach dipped. She did not want Charity hurt the way she had been hurt, perhaps that was why she was being cautious. 'It is far too early to speak of courting, my dear. He and Lady Jersey are friends and by dancing with you he certainly endorsed her decision to give you tickets for Almack's.'

'The patronesses of Almack's actually listen to him?' Patience asked, round-eyed.

'His Grace, Duke of Stone, is respected by every single member of the *ton*.' If he had ignored the girls, it would not have done them any harm. He ignored most people. If he had cut them, their Season would have been over before it began. By dancing with Charity and looking pleased when he returned her to Amelia, by lingering for those few seconds to talk to their chaperon, he had set their feet on the path to wherever they wished to go.

Yet Amelia did not want to stuff their heads with too much nonsense. She did not want them thinking they could do no wrong. A statue could far more easily be knocked off a pedestal then it could be set on high.

Patience finished her hot chocolate. 'Well, duke or no duke, I had a lovely time. I danced almost every set.'

'Much to poor Mr Dobson's chagrin,' Charity said and poked an elbow in her sister's ribs.

'Ouch. Well, at least he didn't leave the way Lord Sherbourn did when he saw you dancing with the Duke.'

That had been a big disappointment for Charity, but she had lifted her chin and danced with every eligible young gentleman Amelia presented.

'Do not worry,' Amelia said. 'He will come around.' Lord Sherbourn was a rather dramatic young man who wore his heart on his sleeve. He had some growing up to do. But he came from good stock and likely this was his first experience of falling in love. It would either endure and become something worth nurturing or it would pass and both young people would move on.

If Sherbourn did not come up to scratch, Amelia had several other young men on her list who would make excellent husbands, some of them higher up in rank than Sherbourn.

She knew better than to look too high. However, with the Duke of Stone's endorsement of Charity, perhaps she had set her sights too low, after all.

'What is it you like about Mr Dobson, anyway, Sister?' Charity asked.

Patience looked thoughtful, then turned pink. 'He doesn't talk about himself non-stop. He asked *me* what I like to do.'

'What did you tell him?' Charity asked, clearly surprised by Patience's hot blush.

'I told him I like picnics. He said he did, too. He is going to ask his mama to arrange one.'

Inwardly, Amelia groaned. Apparently, some sort of outdoor eating was in her not too distant future.

She finished her tea. 'If that is the case, we need to shop for something suitable to wear.'

'Ooh!' squealed Patience. 'More shopping. I love it.'

'Will Lord Sherbourn be invited to the picnic?' Charity sounded a little wistful.

'Since he is a friend of Mr Dobson, I would expect so,' Amelia said.

Charity cheered up. 'Then I really do need a new bonnet.'

Amelia got up. 'Time for bed, ladies, if we are to look our best on the morrow.'

'Will you buy a new bonnet, Mrs Durant?' Charity asked.

'I think I already have something suitable,' Amelia said.

'The Duke might be in attendance,' Charity said, watching her finger trace the pattern on the counterpane.

Amelia stilled. 'And your point is?'

'When you spoke to him, you blushed.'

She opened her mouth to refute the accusation.

'Yes, you did,' Patience said with a giggle.

'I must have been hot,' Amelia said, seeing there was no way to deny the truth. 'As I said, time for bed. We will have a busy day tomorrow.' She quickly made her escape.

Good heavens, did nothing escape those sharp-eyed girls? Clearly, she needed to watch her reactions around the Duke of Stone. If the girls noticed her blushes, others might notice also and get the wrong idea.

Though why she had blushed, she was not sure.

Chapter Three

Later that week, an invitation to a picnic in Greenwich Park arrived at the Mitchells' town house. Both girls were ecstatic, though Patience admitted she had known the invitation was on the way.

'Lady Dobson has a brother in the navy and *he* has a friend who is equerry to the Duke of Clarence who has granted us access to picnic in the park,' Patience had informed Amelia. 'Mr Dobson is hoping he can show me inside the observatory, but he hasn't yet found anyone to sponsor us. Mr Pond allows very few visitors.'

Greenwich Royal Park on the banks of the Thames was also home to the Royal Observatory and the domain of Mr Pond, the Royal Observer.

'It will be too bad if we are unable to go inside,' Patience said.

Apparently, Patience had recently discovered an interest in all things related to the stars and the planets. Perhaps because Mr Dobson was similarly enthralled.

Amelia looked at the invitation that had been thrust at her the moment she arrived at the town house after luncheon. 'It says there will be cricket and croquet and lawn tennis as entertainment after luncheon. Let us hope the weather is fair.'

'Oh, it would be too bad if it is cancelled because of rain,' Patience said.

'We shall just have to wait and see,' Amelia said. 'In the meantime, I see that you ladies are ready for our afternoon drive in the park and, if I am not mistaken, our carriage awaits.'

'The barouche,' Charity said in a tone of disgust.

The sisters had pestered their papa for a fashionable high-perch phaeton. Fortunately, even Papa Mitchell was not doting enough to buy such a dangerous equipage for his daughters, especially since neither of them had any experience driving anything more exciting than a donkey cart.

'A barouche is the perfect carriage for meeting people in Hyde Park,' Amelia said. 'You will see.' She ushered her charges downstairs and out into the street.

The barouche was brand new and beautifully appointed. Fortunately, Papa Mitchell had listened to Amelia when she had told him not to have any sort of crest emblazoned on the sides or anything but the most expensive materials and subdued of colours for the wheels and squabs. It was a picture of understated elegance.

* * *

When they reached Hyde Park the entrance was teaming with both carriages and pedestrians and they had to wait their turn to pass through the gate. Both girls looked charming in their bonnets, spencers and summery gowns, for today was as lovely a spring day as one could wish for on a drive. And that meant the world and his wife were here at the fashionable hour of the promenade.

It was not long before they were greeted by people they had met over the past few weeks. Amelia was proud of how well her charges had been received by the *ton* who made every effort to acknowledge them. With a slight pang, she had to admit some of that was due to the Duke of Stone's condescension at Lady Jersey's ball.

And…there he was, riding towards them. There was no mistaking his broad-shouldered figure in a snug-fitting navy riding coat or his easy masculine carriage. Her heart picked up speed and her stomach fluttered in a most disturbing manner. She took a deep breath and quelled such ridiculousness. She was fearful for the hearts of her charges, that was all, and, knowing the Duke, he had likely forgotten he had ever met them.

She pretended not to see him.

'Oh!' Charity exclaimed, sounding shocked.

Amelia's heart sank, anticipating a snub from Stone.

'There is Lord Sherbourn,' Charity went on. 'I am

sure that is him. Walking with the lady in blue.' She squinted and pouted. 'A very pretty lady.'

Amelia took in the couple. 'Lady Augusta Framton. This is her second Season. I believe her family's estate is close to the Sherbourn home. Likely they are friends.'

Charity twirled her parasol and looked unconvinced. 'He saw me and pretended he did not.'

Oh, dear. Amelia did not like the stubborn set to Charity's chin. She was usually the most obliging of girls, but that particular look often signified she was annoyed and prepared to do something about the issue.

A shadow fell across the carriage. The Duke of Stone had fallen in beside them. 'Good day, ladies,' he said, doffing his tall hat with an elegant bow.

Amelia hid her surprise as they greeted him in turn.

'A fine day for a turn in the park,' he observed when the niceties were concluded.

'It is,' Charity said brightly. She sounded a little brittle to Amelia's ears. 'Nice enough for a picnic. I do hope we are not using up all the good weather so that it rains when we go to Greenwich.'

He gave her an indulgent smile. 'You are attending the Dobsons' party, then?'

Amelia's heart clenched. A sharp little stab of pain that stopped her breath. Was she wrong about Stone? Was he truly interested in Charity? Why else would he have made a point of speaking with them? Perhaps the girl's beauty had turned his head, as it had those of other gentlemen. She took a deep breath to ease the pain in her chest. Papa Mitchell would be thrilled if it was true. It would be the wedding of the Season, should it come to pass.

She just wished she did not have the feeling he would be making a terrible mistake in marrying Charity. No, no. It was Charity she worried for. The Duke was such a cold man and Charity was so sweet, she feared the young woman's spirit might be crushed by the weight of his power.

'We are,' Charity said. 'Patience is hoping to see the telescope in the observatory, but you need a special invitation.'

Stone looked surprised. 'Are you interested in astronomy, Miss Patience?'

'Oh, yes,' Patience said. 'Very much. It doesn't matter if we cannot go into the observatory. Being so close to where Mr Halley made all his observations will be thrilling enough. And I hear the view from there is quite remarkable.'

Oh, dear. Patience was beginning to sound a little too effusive. Hopefully the Duke would not take offence at her youthful enthusiasm, when the fashion was for *ennui*. But from his expression it seemed he was amused rather than disgusted.

'It is, indeed,' he said. 'Let us hope for fine weather. And do you go to Almack's on Wednesday?'

'Yes,' Charity said. 'We received our tickets from Lady Jersey.' She smiled at him shyly. 'I believe we have you to thank for that. I hope I don't break any of the rules.'

'You will not,' Stone said, sounding indulgent. 'Not with Mrs Durant to show you the way.' He nodded at Amelia and heat rushed to her cheeks.

'Thank you, Your Grace,' she said, hoping she sounded normal and not as breathless as she felt. It was idiotic. All the man had done was pay her a commonplace compliment. 'I assume we shall see you there?'

His eyebrows rose and she realised she had sounded rather challenging. Well, it really would be nice to know his purpose for asking, would it not?

He bowed. 'You will indeed.' He turned to Charity. 'May I request a country dance if you have one available?'

For a moment, Charity stared at him, then she nodded firmly. 'I shall be delighted, Your Grace.'

He smiled at her. 'Please, I am Stone to my friends.'

Charity blushed and nodded.

He turned to Patience. 'And may I request the fifth set from you, Miss Patience?'

Patience frowned. 'You want to dance with both of us?'

A quizzical expression crossed his face that Amelia could not interpret. 'I think my aunt would take me to task if I danced with only one of the beautiful Mitchell sisters. It would not be polite.'

Charity tilted her head. 'Is your aunt so strict in her notions, then?'

He chuckled as if sharing a joke known only to the two of them. 'She is indeed, Miss Charity.'

And, clever man, he was being careful not to show

favouritism to one sister or the other. A way of keeping the gossips firmly at bay for his sake and theirs. Amelia had not expected him to be so considerate. Had he changed over the years?

Charity smiled back at him. 'I expect your aunt is like Mrs Durant, then, and knows exactly how one should go on. So, we will follow their instruction and I am sure Patience will be happy to save the fifth set for you.'

He bowed. 'Thank you. I bid you good day, ladies.' He eased his horse away from the carriage and proceeded in the opposite direction.

He had stayed at their side the exact appropriate amount of time to acknowledge their acquaintance-ship without arousing any curiosity, or at least, too much curiosity.

Amelia could not help but admire his *savoir faire*. He was certainly the most polished gentleman she had ever met. Or he was now. When they were younger, she had thought him rather rude.

'There is no denying that man looks exceedingly well on a horse,' Charity said, watching him ride off. 'And I had never noticed before how bright blue his eyes are.'

It seemed the attraction went both ways. Again, her heart gave that painful little squeeze.

Really? She ought to be rejoicing. It seemed very likely she had only one sister left to place.

Travelling through the streets of London with his aunt the following Wednesday evening, Jasper could not recall the last time he had gone to Almack's. He glanced over at his companion. Aunt Mary had been visibly surprised when he asked if she would like him to escort her and visibly thrilled. It wasn't that he disliked dancing, he simply disliked all the trivial conversation that went with it. He always found himself at a loss for words once the formalities were over. And Almack's was at best a dreadful bore. He could not fathom why the ladies liked it so much.

Fortunately, Miss Mitchell chattered on quite happily, leaving one only the necessity of inserting a word or two at the appropriate interval. Besides which, she really was a lovely and sweet girl. Not a mean bone in her body. Perhaps Aunt Mary was right and she would make some man an excellent wife. But would she make him a good duchess?

The carriage slowed and then inched its way towards the front door of the hallowed halls of Almack's assembly rooms. Lady Jersey would not be surprised to see him, but the other hostesses would. And after he danced with them tonight, no one would question the appearance of the Mitchell sisters at all the best parties.

The carriage halted and he helped his aunt down into the street, waited for her while she changed her shoes and escorted her up the stairs to the subscription room. The porter at the door glanced at their tickets and gestured for them to go through. Jasper glanced around. Nothing had changed over the years except perhaps the ladies' fashions.

While he pretended not to notice, he was not unaware of the ripple of his name spreading through the assembled guests. It had been at least three or perhaps four years since he had made an appearance at what was, without doubt, the hub of the marriage mart. It was here that all hopeful mamas paraded their daughters and sons in hopes of catching them a spouse. And that was the reason he had stopped coming. There had been too many caps thrown his way.

He and Aunt Mary joined Lady Jersey and a group of friends a few feet inside the door.

His gaze sought out the Mitchell girls. As usual they were in the middle of a group of fresh-faced young people with their chaperon hovering nearby. He let his gaze pass over them. It would not be good to be seen paying too much attention. He still wasn't sure…

Lady Jersey was observing him with interest, even as she listened to his aunt. When she realised she had his attention, she smiled. 'Is there anyone to whom you wish to be introduced this evening, Duke?'

She was a naughty minx and he'd always liked her for that. He grinned back. 'None at the moment, Sally, thank you, but I anticipate you will keep me supplied with a feast of young women I haven't yet met.'

Sally narrowed her gaze on him. 'And some you have, no doubt.'

He inclined his head. 'Indeed.'

She fluttered her painted fan. 'So, your Aunt Mary is right? You have finally decided to take the idea of marriage seriously?'

He tried not to stiffen at the question. It wasn't impertinence. It was the curiosity of a friend. 'It is high time I settled down and did my duty.'

Aunt Mary shook her head at him. 'You have never been one to shirk your duty, Stone. It is my wish to see you happily settled.'

There it was again, that word. Happy. 'Surrounded by such a plethora of lovely ladies...' he bowed in the two ladies' direction to ensure them they were included in his description '...how could one fail to be happy?'

One of the other men in the group frowned. 'Surrounded by a plethora is about as far away from happy as I could imagine. It is the presence of the person you care about that makes one happy.'

'When did you become such a romantic, Charles?' he said, unable to stop himself from looking down his nose. A reflex. Self-defence. He regretted it the moment he did it.

'When I found my wife,' the man said cheerily.

The couple smiled fondly at each other.

To Jasper's surprise, he found himself envying the look passing between them. The understanding without words. He quelled the unwanted sensation. He did not envy anyone anything. He was glad for anyone who thought themselves happy.

The musicians began the introduction for the next dance and Miss Mitchell was escorted on to the floor by one of her court. Jasper spotted Lady Augusta Framton, who clearly had not yet found herself a partner. 'Excuse me. I need to do my duty and find myself a partner or Sally will have my hide.'

Sally laughed. 'I will indeed.'

He danced with Lady Augusta and with another young lady who Sally brought over to meet him, then went to claim his dance with Miss Charity.

She was standing beside Mrs Durant. Once again, he was struck by the difference in their own particular form of beauty: Miss Mitchell the classic English rose and Mrs Durant as exotic as an orchid.

'Good evening, Stone,' Miss Mitchell said upon his approach.

He bowed. 'How are you enjoying the evening?' He glanced around. 'I saw your sister earlier. She seemed to be in good spirits.'

Miss Mitchell beamed. 'It is exactly as we imagined. I am enjoying myself immensely and so is Patience. The balls at our local assembly were just as crowded, but not nearly as refined.'

He glanced at Mrs Durant, who was smiling fondly at her charge. She had a right to look pleased. The girl was not only lovely, her manners were delightfully free of affectation and the silliness that marked so many of her age.

Once more he had the urge to ask her to dance. He quashed it.

He held out his arm to Miss Mitchell. 'Shall we?'

They strolled on to the dance floor to join the nearest set.

To Amelia, Almack's was proving to be an unmitigated success. The girls had danced every set. Stone had clearly been pleased by both girls and even Mrs

Drummond-Burrell, one of the starchiest of patronesses of Almack's, had unbent enough to compliment her on the demeanours of the girls. She'd also congratulated her on setting their feet on the path to making extraordinarily good matches.

Soon her task would be done. So why was she not pleased?

Given the girls' beauty and the wealth of their papa, Amelia had not expected to have any difficulty finding suitable husbands for the sisters, but Stone? And Charity? Something about it was making her feel uncomfortable. Never before had she felt so worried about a match she had arranged.

Nothing Stone had done or said led her to believe he meant Charity harm, but one careless word from him, one small indiscretion by her, could ruin the young woman's reputation for ever more. Men did as they pleased and women trod warily. It wasn't fair, but it was the way of the world.

When the girls took tea in Almack's antechamber set aside for the purpose, Stone had not joined them and their friends, but instead had been seated with his aunt, Lady Mary, and Sally Jersey. Amelia had joined Lady Dobson and some of the other matrons while keeping a close eye on her charges. One of the matrons had approached her about finding her son a wife. Amelia did not usually take on young gentlemen, but had, after the woman pleaded with her, agreed to consider making an exception.

After supper there would be waltzing, but both sisters would sit out, although Sally had said she would approve of them dancing, if Amelia wished. Amelia had thought it better to wait until they had been in society a little longer, especially since she had not had an opportunity to observe them in the dance. It turned into a sad romp if it was not done properly with the right partner.

'May I have this dance?' a deep voice said beside her.

She started. 'Your Grace?' Her heart tumbled over. No. No, she must have misheard. 'I beg your pardon, I was wool-gathering.' She frowned. 'You did not just ask me—?'

'At the risk of being refused yet again, I did.'

People were looking at them and he was holding out his arm, making it impossible for her to refuse without seeming rude.

'Very well.'

'Do you have to look so cross about it?'

Indignant at the accusation, but worried he might be right, she smiled. 'You took me by surprise. I suppose you asked Charity and she told you she does not yet have permission.'

'I did not.'

'Oh, but—'

He raised both eyebrows.

She put her hand on his sleeve and they strolled on to the dance floor.

No one would call Amelia diminutive. She was a little above the average height for a woman and, while most men were an inch or two taller, the Duke made her feel small and feminine. Perhaps that was what had attracted her to him all those years ago. She pushed the thought aside. Back then she had been young and full of romantic notions. She now saw the world through the eyes of experience and, in her experience, romance wilted faster than roses. Suitability and compatibility were far more important than sentiment.

She was not sure why Stone had asked her to dance, but perhaps it was part of his strategy to ensure she favoured his suit with Charity. Why would she not? And Charity's father would be exceedingly pleased, but deep in her heart she had trouble believing that the remote Duke of Stone was suitable for a young lively girl like Charity.

The music began and for the first few seconds she focused on her steps and becoming used to her partner. It had been a long time since she had waltzed, but she need not have worried. He danced beautifully and, with such manly athletic grace, it was easy to relax and let him lead.

'You waltz better than most ladies I have danced with.'

She frowned. 'You flatter me, Your Grace.'

'I do not flatter, Mrs Durant. It is not in my nature.'

'Then I thank you for the compliment.'

She glanced up and was surprised to find that while his face retained its usual expression of cool detachment, his blue eyes were dancing with amusement.

'What is the jest?'

His lips twitched as if he was holding back a smile.

'No jest. I do wonder, however, what I have done for you to take me in dislike.'

She started and he somehow caught her before she stumbled and swung her into a turn beneath his arm. At the conclusion of the move they were face to face and exceedingly close. Close enough for her to inhale his bay-scented cologne and see the faint haze of dark stubble on his square chin. She really liked the firm set of his jaw. It showed character and purpose.

She collected her wandering thoughts. 'I have not taken you in dislike, Your Grace.'

'Stone, if you please.'

She nodded at his inclusion of her in his circle of friends, though she was sure his closest friends likely called him Jasper.

'But you are reserving judgement,' he said as he turned her and then glided down the length of the room with his hand firmly on her waist. There was nothing improper about his touch, but every nerve in her body seemed to tingle with awareness.

'Not at all.' She would be glad when this dance was over. Would she not?

'One hates to argue with a lady, but the expression on your face says otherwise. For some reason, I make you nervous. We met before, did we not? I have a faint memory that eludes me in detail.'

She gazed at him, surprised. Even a faint memory was more than she had expected. Unless he had pretended not to recognise her the second time they met. 'There is nothing to recall.'

He tilted his head. 'Was I so unremarkable, then?'

Dash it all. He was not going to be satisfied. 'We met the year I came out.'

His brow furrowed slightly. 'And?'

'And nothing. We were introduced. We did not speak again.'

'Was I rude?'

'You were yourself.'

He twirled around and back again. 'So, I was rude.'

'It does not matter, Stone. It was years ago. Before I was married.'

'If it did not matter, then you would not still be… annoyed.'

They reached at the end of the room and he guided her around several couples who were making a hash of the turn.

'I am not annoyed.' She huffed out a breath. 'I will admit, I was not impressed by the haughtiness of your manner, but it is or should be long forgotten.'

'I see. You know, when I inherited the dukedom, it did not take me long to realise that many of those offering friendship were drawn to me by the idea of the title. I admit to being a little standoffish.'

'Only a little?' She gave him a quizzical look.

'Very well. Very standoffish. Wary of all except those I knew to be my good friends.'

Heat attacked her cheeks as she recalled her mortification at the moment he had looked down his nose at her and moved on. 'It is good to see you coming out of your shell at last, then.' Her voice sounded a little more tart that she had intended.

His lips flattened. 'I see that I caused you great

offence.' The music ended and he offered her his escort, returning her to the corner of the room where her charges awaited.

'It is water under the bridge,' she said. 'I scarcely recall it.'

'Then there is no more to be said.' His voice was chilly.

He bowed to the girls and sauntered away. She watched him go with an odd feeling in her chest. A painful sense of regret that she had not been a little kinder.

'Mrs Durant, Lord Sherbourn wants to know if he can dance with me again. He said as long as no more than two—'

'I thought all your dances were spoken for.'

'They are.'

'Then there is your answer. Once you have agreed to dance you cannot go back on your word. It would not be polite.'

'I expect if it was the Duke of Stone who wanted a second dance with me, you would find a way to arrange it.'

She stared at Charity in surprise. 'Of course I would not. What would make you say such a thing?'

Charity sighed. 'Because you want me to marry him. You and Papa.'

'I think it is far too soon to be talking of marriage to anyone,' she said briskly.

The young man who had engaged Charity for the next dance arrived at her elbow.

'Miss Mitchell, are you ready for our dance? I hope you like the quadrille,' he said. 'It is my favourite.'

For a moment Amelia thought the easy-going girl might dig in her heels, but she smiled sweetly at the young man. 'I do like it.' She went off with her partner seeming happy enough, but left Amelia with a feeling of foreboding.

Perhaps Amelia should warn Stone off. Tell him that Charity's feelings were engaged elsewhere.

She froze. What would Mr Mitchell say if she did any such thing? And what if she was wrong? Surely Charity could not prefer Lord Sherbourn over the Duke of Stone? What if Stone's emotions were truly engaged? He would be terrible hurt to be rejected for the likes of Sherbourn. The idea of Charity causing him pain gave her a little stab in her heart.

Perhaps when Charity got to know the Duke better, she would see his true worth.

It was clearly her duty to help open her eyes. Duty was not always a kind master.

Chapter Four

The day for the promised picnic at Greenwich Royal Park dawned clear and fine. A perfect day in late May. Lady Dobson's invitation had made it clear that if there was even a hint of rain in the morning, then the event would be postponed because, as she had remarked to Amelia, soggy hems and wet shoes were no fun at all.

When the girls had expressed their anxiety about the weather, Papa Mitchell had offered to provide an awning large enough to accommodate every member of the *ton*. He had trouble understanding that he could not simply step in and take over the arrangements for someone else's party. It simply wasn't done. Fortunately, no such intervention needed to be contemplated or warded off.

The drive from London to Greenwich did not take very long and they arrived at eleven, an unusually early start for members of the *ton*. The guests were met at the gate by liveried footmen who led them up the hill to an open area where their host and hostess awaited them.

Lady Dobson looked magnificent in a purple-and-black-striped silk gown and a fetching bonnet adorned with purple fruits. She greeted them genially. Lord Dobson, a small balding man who wore a straw hat, seemed content to remain in his wife's shadow once he had shaken hands.

'Harold,' Lady Dobson said, calling her son over. 'Please show the Misses Mitchell where to leave their shawls. Perhaps they would like to play croquet?'

The young Mr Dobson took charge of Charity and Patience. Once Amelia saw they were happily engaged with their usual group of friends, she relaxed. The party was not a large one, given the logistics of bringing necessary chairs, tables and food all the way from London, and consisted mostly of those newly out this Season and their parents, about thirty guests in all.

'It is very brave of you to undertake a picnic so far from home,' Amelia remarked to Lady Dobson, taking in the tables covered in bright white cloths, neatly set and each with a floral arrangement as a centrepiece.

'My butler is a genius at this sort of thing,' Lady Dobson said. 'To be honest, if Harold had not been so keen to show the observatory to Miss Patience, I likely would not have attempted it.'

The observatory, further up the hill behind them, was enclosed by a wall. 'Do you have permission for the guests to go inside?'

Lady Dobson sighed. 'No. Lord Dobson tried, but Mr Pond was too busy with his observations and could not be reached. We must simply be satisfied with the view, I suppose.'

The view across the park to the river was indeed magnificent. In the foreground, at the bottom of the hill, the Queen's House built for Anne of Denmark by James I was one of the first classical buildings ever built in England. Beyond it lay the Thames. The sails of ships large and small, plying their way up to London or heading down river to the sea, added to the beauty of the scene. Far in the distance, amid the haze, one could pick out the myriad church spires of London.

'And we have a surprise planned for later,' Lady Dobson said, looking quite mysterious. 'To make up for not being able to go into the observatory.' She raised a hand. 'Don't ask me about it. It is all Harold's doing and he will not tell me a thing. I will accept neither credit or criticism, however it turns out.'

Amelia could only hope the young man hadn't thought up anything shocking or dangerous. 'I look forward to it.'

'Oh, he did come,' Lady Dobson said, sounding startled and nervous. 'I thought Harold was teasing me when he said Stone intended to join us. It seems Harold and the Duke have become fast friends.' Amelia spun around, her heart picking up speed. She had not seen the Duke of Stone since their waltz at Almack's. He had not been at any of the other events they had attended the previous week and Amelia had decided that his kindness to the girls had merely been to please Sally Jersey. And their waltz? Merely a way of amusing himself at her expense.

'Dobson,' Lady Dobson said to her husband, 'come and greet the Duke of Stone.' She hurried off, her husband in tow. Grinning widely, the young Mr Dobson also hurried to greet their ducal visitor.

Stone strode up the hill, not in his usual formal dark coat, but rather looking every inch the country gentleman in breeches, an olive-green riding coat and high-topped boots. If she wasn't mistaken he was also wearing the Four Horse Club neckerchief around his throat. He looked more relaxed, more comfortable than she could have imagined in a man so reserved, though there was no mistaking the nobility of his bearing.

She shook her head at her desire to see only the best in him. After all, he walked up that hill as if knowing no wayward fleck of mud would dare mar the mirror-like polish of his boots, though the wind was actually daring enough to ruffle his carefully ordered locks as he removed his hat to make his bow to their hostess. If he was aware of the disruption of his inimitable style, he ignored it, unlike some of the other young gentlemen who were consistently pushing and combing with their fingers at wind-tossed locks.

The Duke's long stride soon brought him up to the Dobsons. He greeted them, looking about him much as Amelia had done. His gaze caught hers and he bowed. She blushed at being found staring, but she dipped a curtsy and smiled.

She was pleased he had not decided to take her in dislike after their frank conversation about their first meeting. She would hate for her honesty to harm Charity and Patience's prospects.

Aware that he might think she was listening in on his conversation with his hosts, she wandered a little further up the hill to see if a higher elevation offered a different perspective.

Strangely, she felt the need to compose herself, to give her heart time to settle into its usual calm rhythm, before she spoke with Stone.

At the top, close to the Observatory wall, she turned to take in the view. To her surprise, Stone was following in her footsteps. He smiled as he reached her side 'Trying to avoid me, Mrs Durant?'

'Goodness me, no,' she said, feeling breathless and hoping he would put it down to her climb. 'I simply wanted to see more of this extraordinary vista. I had heard of it, of course, but have never been here.'

'It is something, isn't it,' he said, turning to look out over the countryside.

'Lady Dobson says you and her son Harold have become good friends?'

'He is a pleasant enough young fellow and seems to have a brain.' Stone agreed. 'Despite—' He broke off.

'Despite his less than awe-inspiring appearance, were you going to say? I believe what is inside a person's mind is more important that the outward shell, don't you?'

He nodded. 'I do indeed.'

Should she believe that? Or was he simply trying to curry favour with Charity, by agreeing with her chaperon?

The latter seemed unlikely. Stone did not need anyone's approval and he knew it.

Jasper tried not to show his irritation at Mrs Durant's obvious set down. He had tried to come to some sort of truce at Almack's, but it seemed he remained in her bad books. Did that bode ill for the favour he had to ask of her? He could ask someone else, he supposed, but she seemed to be the most appropriate person.

What? Was he hesitating because he cared that she might refuse? If she did, it would make no difference. He had alternatives.

'Have you been inside the Observatory?' he said by way of opening the topic.

'I have not.' She glanced up at the roof of the building where the telescopes were housed. 'I must say, it seems less imposing than I expected. It was designed by Sir Christopher Wren, I understand.'

'It was. King Charles didn't give him much to work with, however. I gather they built it with the stones from the castle that stood here originally. It is certainly more functional than beautiful.'

'King Charles had other uses for his funds, I suppose.'

'Given the importance of the observations to shipping you would have thought he would have been a great deal more generous,' he agreed. 'Still, Mr Pond has things well in hand. The accuracy of the clocks here are a marvel.'

She looked surprised. 'You seem to know a great deal about it.'

'It is my duty to know about it—I am a member of the Board of Visitors as my father was before me. Besides, I have a vested interest. The success of my shipping investments depends upon it.'

'I see.'

'Which brings me to the reason I wished to speak to you.'

She glanced up at him, surprise in her gaze. And perhaps a shade of disappointment. What? Had she thought he had sought her out for the pleasure of her company? His heart lightened for some peculiar reason.

'I have obtained permission for Mr Dobson and Miss Patience to visit the observatory. However, I cannot allow them to wander around by themselves. It would not be seemly.'

'Certainly not,' she said.

'Nor would it be seemly for them to go with only me for a chaperon, so I wondered if you would care to make one of the party? I know it is not all that exciting, but Dobson had his heart set on it.'

'So did Patience, though she would never say so. She will be thrilled to hear that she is to go inside. Of course, I will be delighted to accompany her.'

'And Mr Dobson.'

'Yes.' She gave a slightly laugh, a lovely musical sound. 'Him, too.'

'Good. That is settled. We should go before afternoon tea is served, since Lady Dobson says something else is planned for later.'

'She is being very mysterious about it, too,' Mrs Durant said. 'Did she give you any hint?'

He frowned at the hint of worry in her voice. 'I did not think to ask her.'

'Well, it is of no matter.'

If it was of no matter, why had she brought it up? 'Shall we go and tell Dobson the good news?'

At that she laughed. 'You have not told him yet?'

'I did not. I wanted to be certain I had your agreement before I went letting the cat out of the bag. Nothing is more likely to stir the pot than me offering a treat which does not have your approval.'

'I appreciate your consideration.'

Did she? The idea that she might pleased him.

He offered his arm to guide her down the hill and she took it, resting her hand on his sleeve so lightly he could not feel it through the fabric of his coat. He liked that she did not try to clutch at him the way some young ladies did. Yet with her, he would not have minded if she leaned on him a bit more.

Harold Dobson grinned when he saw them approaching. 'You two make a very handsome couple,' he observed.

Mrs Durant stiffened, but did not respond, or even

show on her face that she had heard what the young man had said. 'The Duke has some news for you.'

The young man pushed his hair out of his eyes and peered at Jasper. 'Are you offering me the job as your secretary? I did not think you planned to let me know until next week.'

'I will let you know next week, as I said before. Today, I am offering you a visit to the Observatory, courtesy of Mr Pond.'

Miss Patience's face lit up. 'Truly?'

Jasper nodded.

'I say, that is capital.' Dobson beamed.

'When do we go?' Miss Patience asked.

'Now would be best,' he said. 'I already have your chaperon's approval.'

'How wonderful,' Miss Patience said. 'What about Charity? May she come also?'

'Four people is all I have permission for. If you think your sister would be interested, I would be happy to bring her another time.'

Patience shook her head. 'If you want to please my sister, you would do better to take her driving. She is not really interested in the stars.'

Yes, he could imagine that Miss Mitchell would by far prefer a turn around the park in his phaeton. 'Then let us be off.'

With the younger members of the party rushing ahead of them, he escorted Mrs Durant up the hill at a more leisurely pace. He liked the way her stride, while not as long as his own natural gate, was easy to match. He liked the feel of her hand on his arm. He was tempted to cover that elegant gloved hand with his own, the need for a gesture of possession he did not understand. At the gate, with Miss Patience practically hopping up and down in an impatience that made him want to laugh, he handed the man on duty his calling card and they were admitted with alacrity.

The porter led them across the cobblestone courtyard. 'To the west are the apartments of the Astronomer Royal,' the porter announced. 'If you would be so good as to follow me?' He led them left, to a range of low old-fashioned buildings with picturesque gables and roughly tiled roofs.

Mrs Durant frowned. 'It is even worse than I thought.'

'Truly awful,' he said.

'You do not know how much I appreciate this, Duke,' Dobson said, coming alongside. 'My cousin, the Admiral, was not able to convince Mr Pond to let us in. He does not approve of sightseers, apparently.'

Admirals and dukes were two very different animals. As a member of the Board of Visitors, Stone, with others, was actually responsible for the oversight of the Observatory. 'As long as we don't break anything, I am sure you will be welcome to return from time to time.'

'My word, I would like that.'

The porter led them through a doorway into a room with a large instrument at its centre.

'This is the Transit Circle Room,' the porter announced.

A gentleman who was working at a desk glanced

up. One of the mathematicians employed by Mr Pond, he clearly recognised Jasper, since he got to his feet, came to meet them and bowed. 'Your Grace, welcome to Flamsteed House. It has been quite a while since your last visit.'

'It has,' Jasper agreed. He introduced his companions and glanced at his watch. 'I believe we are not too late?'

'No, indeed. I am preparing now.' He turned to Dobson with a smile. 'I understand you are interested in seeing how we make our observations. I am about to undertake those taken every day at noon. Would you care to join me?'

He led them over to the large telescope in the centre of the room. 'This is our transit instrument. It was built by Mr Troughton for our previous Royal Observer, Mr Maskelyne. It allows us to correctly measure distances in the heavens.'

After listening to the young man's explanations, Mrs Durant left his side to wander around the room.

'You do not wish to observe?' he asked her.

'I thought to give them a little space,' she said, indicating the young couple taking it in turns to look through the telescope.

'That is thoughtful of you.' He glanced back at the couple. 'Miss Patience has an enquiring mind.'

Amelia tensed at the Duke's statement. She could not tell if he was displeased or otherwise by his tone. She had noticed that most men were intimidated if a woman showed too much intelligence. She forced herself to speak calmly. 'I hope you do not hold that against her?'

'Not at all. Intelligence and beauty. It is a delightful combination. Clearly, Dobson appreciates it. The older sister is the more beautiful of the two, though. And far more pliable in her personality.'

The Duke would no doubt prefer a woman who would not question him at every turn. 'Indeed.' Oh, dear. That sounded a little repressive. 'She is very pleasant company.' It seemed he, like many other men, preferred beauty to brains. Likely the reason he had looked down his nose at her all those years ago.

On that front, he might be disappointed. While Charity did not have quite the sharp mind of her sister, she was nobody's fool and not always 'pliant'.

The Duke pointed up at a large telescope hung on a wall. 'That is the first fixed-transit instrument used here at Greenwich. Put in by Halley. Over there is the great mural quadrant built by Graham.' He indicated a huge metal arc divided into a series of measurements with a pointer suspended from its right-hand corner like the hand of a clock.

A series of oohs and ahs from the young couple at the telescope drew their attention. Patience stepped back from the eyepiece and Dobson took her place. Patience smiled at the young mathematician. 'Thank you so much. That was the most interesting thing I have ever seen, I think.'

The young gentleman beamed, clearly dazzled by the beauty who was smiling at him so charmingly, flushed red and tugged at his cravat. 'Perhaps you would like to see the circle room built by Mr Halley during his term as Royal Astronomer.' He walked them to a door in the east wall.

Amelia glanced at the Duke and was surprised to find his gaze fixed on her face. A hot flush rose up from her chest all the way to her hairline, as if the warmth in his eyes had somehow heated her skin. Why was he looking at her in that way? 'We should go with them,' she said weakly.

He grimaced slightly. 'There was something else I wanted to show you.'

She hesitated. What harm could Patience come to with two respectable young men? Besides, Patience was not the sort to encourage any nonsense. 'Very well.'

He tucked her hand beneath his arm and his touch sent a trickle of heat drifting along her veins. She gasped.

He looked down. 'Is something wrong?'

'No, not at all.' She swallowed, trying to relieve the dryness in her mouth. She could not understand this effect he had on her. Not one bit. 'What is it you wanted to show me?'

'This.' He pointed to yet another telescope. 'This one is the instrument Bradley used when he discovered the aberration of light. The final incontrovertible proof the earth moves around the sun.'

This was clearly something he cared about. This observatory and its observations and its history. It seemed he was passionate about something, after all, not at all as removed from ordinary emotions as she had supposed.

'You believe in this,' she said.

'I do. It is vital. Every step forward means fewer losses at sea. To an island nation like ours it is imperative.'

The intensity in his voice sent a shiver down her spine. 'Your interests in shipping must be huge.'

His mouth tightened. 'I was fifteen when my parents were on a ship that ran aground. With more accuracy with regard to the ship's position, it might not have occurred.'

Understanding dawned. A pang struck her heart. 'I am so sorry. I had no idea.'

He stiffened. 'It is not something of which I like to speak.'

The remoteness returned his voice, as if he realised he had said more than he had intended. Clearly, he did not want her sympathy. An awkward silence ensued.

Voices from the other room drifted through the open door on the other side of the room. 'Oh, dear, we are supposed to be acting as chaperons. We really ought to go and make sure everything is going as it should.'

Inside that next chamber, a huge telescope pointed skywards. Their guide was showing Patience and Dobson how it could be moved in a circle to observe any part of the sky.

The Duke glanced at his watch. 'I promised Lady Dobson we would be back in time for our meal and I am sure our guide has other things to do.'

Patience looked ready to argue, but Mr Dobson nodded at the Duke. 'You are right, Your Grace. This visit has been vastly interesting, but my mother, after all her hard work, will not be happy if we are late.' He offered his arm to Patience.

The young mathematician bowed. 'It has been a great pleasure to show you and your guests around the Royal Observatory, Your Grace. Mr Pond will be most gratified in your interest.' He ushered them to the door and they stepped out into the courtyard where the porter waited to show them out.

They wandered down the hill to where the guests were indeed gathering at the tables.

The Duke joined their host and hostess while Mr Dobson led Amelia and Patience to a table full of young people and their chaperons. Amelia glanced over at Stone and saw that he was listening to Lord Dobson with his usual distant expression and she wondered if he was regretting his generosity to the young Mr Dobson. He certainly did not look as if he was enjoying himself. But then he rarely did. This morning had been an unusual unbending of that icy exterior.

And she had still not figured out his motive, since Charity was not with them, therefore had no opportunity to view his kindness.

She frowned. Perhaps he hoped Patience would put in a good word for him with Charity. Was he less confident than he appeared?

Thinking of Charity—where was she? It took a moment or two to discover her whereabouts. Amelia frowned at the sight of her charge sitting at a table for two with only Lord Sherbourn for company.

She glanced over at the Duke. Had he noticed? Since he had his back to where Charity was sitting, Amelia assumed not. Good Lord, it did not matter whether the Duke had noticed or not. Every other lady present would have seen her in what looked like a private *tête-à-tête*. While they were surrounded by guests, it simply was not done for a single young lady like Charity to behave in such a harum-scarum fashion. It would certainly give rise to gossip.

'I am going to sit with your sister,' she said to Patience. As much as she would have liked to hurry, she sauntered to where the young couple were seated, taking care not to look anxious.

A few feet shy of her target, a slim woman in Pomona green accosted her. 'Mrs Durant. Good day to you.' There was nothing friendly in the greeting.

Amelia cursed inwardly, but smiled and dipped a curtsy. 'Lady Warkworth. How lovely to meet you again.'

Lady Warkworth's daughter, Janet, had been quite friendly with Charity and Patience when they first came to town, but more recently she had avoided their company. Amelia had thought Janet a very nice, but rather plain, young woman and had not been surprised when she deliberately distanced herself from the two beautiful sisters. They really did throw her into the shade in looks and conversation.

'You should not permit Miss Mitchell to sit with

that young man in that intimate way. It is most unseemly.'

Amelia stiffened at the note of censure in the woman's voice. 'I believe Lord Sherbourn should know better than to draw a young lady aside in that particular way, don't you? It is not his first Season, after all.'

Lady Warkworth bridled. 'Young men will do what comes into their heads, but a well-bred young woman would know better. And if you were a proper chaperon, instead of gallivanting off with the Duke and making a cake of yourself, you would ensure the young lady in your charge was observing the proprieties.'

Amelia's jaw dropped at both the slight on Charity and on herself. 'I beg your pardon?'

'Oh, I know what you are about. Setting your own cap at the Duke while you catch a viscountcy for a cit's daughter.'

The venom in the woman's voice shocked Amelia into silence.

'You think yourself so clever,' Lady Warkworth continued, 'but mark my words, the Sherbourns are looking much higher than Miss Mitchell for their son.'

'Higher, like your own daughter, for instance.'

'Well, why not? Our family is exceedingly well connected. We are related to the royal family. And you need not think Stone has any intention of marrying an ageing widow. I do hear he is looking for a mistress, now his previous one has moved on.'

Stunned, she stared at lady Warkworth. 'I can assure you I have no interest in—'

'Then you had better make sure you are not seen so much in his company, Mrs Durant. Everyone is talking about how cosy you and he seem and how cleverly you have cut out the older Mitchell sister.' She nodded briskly and moved away.

Everyone thought she was setting her cap at the Duke? Or that she was trying to lure him into some sort of *arrangement*? She should have guessed the gossips would have a field day after their waltz.

To assume she would be so underhanded as to try to snare her client's potential bridegroom was an insult that was not to be borne. She would make sure no one could say that about her again. Anger heating her veins, she marched over to the young couple, whose attention was wholly devoted to each other.

When her shadow fell across the table, the pair looked up and started. As they should.

'Charity, please join your sister and me at our table.'

The girl's blue eyes widened. She glanced at Lord Sherbourn. 'Charlie invited me to sit with him for luncheon.'

Amelia gave the young man a stern look. 'I would think a gentleman would have more care for your reputation.'

Sherbourn flushed scarlet and looked ready to argue. Amelia raised an eyebrow and he wilted. 'Go and sit with your sister, Miss Mitchell,' he mumbled. Stiffly, he helped Charity to rise, then bowed. 'I will see you later.' He sauntered away, trying to appear perfectly at ease.

Amelia shook her head. 'Lord Sherbourn really should know better, Charity, and so should you. Since I cannot trust you to know how to go on, from now on you will remain with me and your sister.'

The hurt in Charity's eyes made Amelia feel like a dragon. Well, that was what she was, wasn't it? A dragon protecting the very fragile reputations of the two young ladies in her charge.

Chapter Five

Jasper was surprised at how much he was enjoying the picnic. He'd spent years avoiding events such as this. In the first year of his come out, he'd been a target for every matchmaking mama and calculating beauty who had arrived in London. And despite Aunt Mary's dire warnings, he had actually thought they liked him. In his second Season, feeling quite the experienced man, he had fallen at the feet of that Season's beauty, like every other young man on the town. He had been so sure she felt the same way as he did. She made him feel like a god among men. He'd been on the verge of proposing when she begged him to find another on whom to lavish his attentions. She'd explained that if he made her an offer she would have no choice but to accept. She preferred another man, but her parents would never let her refuse a duke.

He'd been shocked by his inability to recognise that her seeming pleasure in his company was false. Not to mention how devastated he was by her rejection. Later he'd decided he had had a lucky escape and had put aside his foolish romantic notions. The experience had taught him to avoid toadies and sycophants and sweetly smiling ladies. His immense power made people behave strangely indeed. He'd learned now not to trust appearances and to freeze all feelings from his communications with people great or small.

His dealings with Albert Carling had been further proof that when others looked at him, they saw not a man, but a title and a means to an end.

When the time came, his choice of a bride would be based on reason, not passion. So why did he find himself drawn to the exotic Mrs Durant? A woman who, while polite, kept her distance. Perhaps that was the reason for his attraction. He was used to people currying his favour and she was a refreshing change.

It was as if she had thrown down a gauntlet and challenged him to make her like him. It made no sense for him to pick up her glove. She was not the sort of woman he ought to be thinking about. Her goal was to marry him off to one of the Mitchell girls and collect her fee.

'It is a very good investment, Your Grace,' Lord Dobson was saying. 'Solid as a rock. Men whom I respect greatly are convinced this is the way of the future.'

Jasper forced his attention back to his host. 'Steam engines have proven to be unreliable, my lord. A novelty. Like hot air balloons.' He actually agreed with

Lord Dobson about the possibilities for steam, but he was not about put his blunt down on any old horse.

Dobson leaned back, in his chair, his expression one of a man about to deliver a great truth. 'I'll agree, there are improvements to be made, Your Grace. I view it as a long-term investment. The important fact to make note of is that there are only two things needed for a steam engine to run.' He delivered this last as if it was a tablet from the mount.

'Water and coal,' Jasper said. 'And I own the largest coal mine in England.'

Dobson sat up straight. 'I see Your Grace is on top of things. But there is something more. Something you should think about. Gas lighting, Your Grace.'

Coal produced gas. 'Perhaps this is a matter we should discuss at another time, in private,' Jasper said. The table where Mrs Durant and her party were sitting was breaking up. He had finished his own meal some moments ago.

He caught himself. Had he really intended to follow the woman like some lovesick swain? No. It was not possible. He merely did not like discussing business at a social event. It simply was not done.

'As you wish, Your Grace. I will have my man of business contact yours and arrange a meeting for tomorrow,' Lord Dobson said. 'Strike while the iron is hot is my motto. You won't want to find yourself missing out on this venture. Not when you hear the whole of it, I'll bet my best boots.'

Jasper found himself amused, rather than irritated, by the man's enthusiasm. 'I shall be pleased to look into this investment opportunity of yours in greater detail. Have your man send over the details before the meeting.'

Lord Dobson looked pleased and gratified.

Lady Dobson on the other hand was looking anxious. 'Oh, my word, what has Harold done now?'

'What concerns you, my dear?' Dobson turned in the direction of his wife's shocked stare. As did Jasper. He repressed the urge to laugh. It would not be polite given his hostess's obvious distress.

Across the lawn marched a ragtag group of mummers, men dressed as women or in other guises including a dragon and a knight, with the clear intention of performing a play.

The guests rose from the tables or left the games they'd been playing and gathered around them in a semi-circle.

Jasper joined Mrs Durant, who frowned and somehow managed to move so he was beside Miss Mitchell rather than herself. The girl smiled up at him. 'Isn't this fun? I have never seen a mummers' play before.'

'Then you are in for a treat.'

Miss Mitchell gave him an enquiring glance.

Lady Dobson coloured, shook her head, bit her lip and rushed off to speak to her son. After some sort of argument, Lady Dobson looked resigned and returned to her place beside Jasper.

'Harold promises me it won't be shockingly bawdy,' Lady Dobson said in a low voice. 'I do apologise, Your Grace.'

As the play unfolded, their audience broke into

loud laughter at the death of the knight, at his miraculous cure by the capering doctor and his final slaying of the dragon with much feinting and dodging. At the end, the players looked very pleased with the applause they received.

Jasper expected them to come around begging for payment as was traditional, but they did not. In fact, as they moved off he caught a few words they spoke among themselves and he realised these were not common folks at all.

'They are very good. Who are they?' he asked Lady Dobson.

She pursed her lips as if unwilling to say, then sighed. 'Harold's friends from university. Not exactly gentlemen. They did it to raise funds for their education while at Cambridge.'

'Yet they do not ask for alms.'

'No, they played as a favour for my son.'

The young Mr Dobson was a man of many parts. With the right sort of encouragement, he would go far.

From time to time during the play, Jasper had glanced at Mrs Durant and she, too, had obviously enjoyed the mummery of the players. More than once, she had laughed out loud at some naughty joke or political reference.

He liked watching her laugh. Most of the time she was far too serious.

He moved to stand beside her, received a discouraging glance and ignored it. What on earth had he done now? Whatever it was, he intended to find out.

But here was not the time or the place to get to the bottom of her annoyance.

'I see that you enjoyed the play,' he said.

'I did. I haven't seen mummers perform since I was a child.'

'What about the theatre—do you enjoy that also?'

'I do, though it is some time since I attended.'

About to invite her, he hesitated. She would refuse. 'What about the Misses Mitchell? Do they enjoy the theatre?'

She turned to face him. 'They do, I believe.'

'You believe? Then I gather they have not been since they come to London.'

'I have suggested to their papa that he rent a box, but he has not done so as yet.'

'Then do me the honour of accepting an invitation to use my box next Friday evening. I will transport you in my carriage.'

'I do not think—'

'Shall I speak to Mr Mitchell? Perhaps his permission is required?'

She narrowed her eyes in suspicion.

He maintained an expression of innocent enquiry.

'I am sure Charity and Patience will be delighted to accompany you to the theatre,' she said. 'Will Lady Mary serve as chaperon?'

He almost chuckled at this little ploy of hers. 'My aunt will not be in town next week. She has planned a visit to friends in Bath.' Or she would have one planned after he spoke to her.

'I see.'

'So, you will do me the great honour of joining my party?'

'We will.'

Her unwilling agreement made him want to laugh when he should have been annoyed. But he thought he knew why she was being so elusive. He was absolutely certain she felt the attraction that sparked between them and she was doing everything in her power to resist its allure.

How could he possibly not recall their first meeting? Could she have invented it as a way of reeling him in? The thought left a bitter taste in his mouth.

In Amelia's opinion, the evening at the theatre rolled around all too quickly. It seemed the girls felt the same way.

'I do not see why we must attend the theatre with the Duke,' Charity grumbled and she turned this way and that, regarding her reflection in the long mirror in the room the girls shared. 'I would much rather go to my first play with Lord Sherbourn.'

'So would I,' Patience said. 'Then we could have invited Mr Dobson.'

Amelia also wished she was not going. Oh, dear, this was not an auspicious start to what should have been a wonderful evening. It was ages since she had attended the theatre and if it had been with anyone else...

What was she thinking? This was a perfect opportunity for Charity to get to know the Duke better. To see his good qualities. To realise his worth. A pang in her chest made her catch her breath. What? Was she jealous? Surely not? She was simply concerned that Charity not make a dreadful mistake, the way she had.

Did that mean she was wrong in encouraging his suit? Should she speak of her reservations to Charity's papa? And if Stone decided it was Charity he wanted? How would a mere mortal like her stand in his way? Never had she felt so conflicted about one of her matches before.

She retied the bow in Charity's hair and stepped back to regard the result. Any man would have to be pleased with the way Charity looked. Young and lovely, yes, but also with a quiet sort of confidence.

'Firstly,' Amelia said, 'the Sherbourns do not own a box or yet rent one for the Season, so they cannot invite us. Secondly, it is very good of the Duke to include us in his party. To turn him down would be rude.' She hoped her own feelings of concern were not apparent in her tone. Oh, how she wished Lady Mary had not gone to Bath and left her acting as chaperon.

Being around Stone made her uncomfortable. But this evening was not about her, it was about these girls and their futures.

She regarded Patience with a critical eye. 'My dear, is that a hole in your glove?'

Patience flushed and tucked her hands behind her back. 'I pulled at a thread.'

'Go and ask your maid for another pair,' Amelia said.

'All this fuss just because he is a duke.' Patience disappeared into the dressing room.

'No, Patience,' Amelia said raising her voice a fraction. 'A well-bred young lady does not leave her house with holes in her gloves, any more than she would leave her house in a moth-eaten shawl. I hope you both have a paper of pins in your reticules in case some mishap should occur once we depart.'

'Yes,' they chorused.

Patience returned at the same moment the knocker sounded and they went down and boarded the waiting carriage.

The Duke met them at the theatre and opened the carriage door when they pulled up at the kerb. He bowed them out of the carriage, looking positively delicious in his evening clothes. Amelia winced inwardly at her instant reaction. What was the matter with her?

'Good evening, ladies,' he said.

Amelia glanced around. Where was the rest of his party? They must already have gone to his box.

In the lobby, the patrons were slowly making their way to their appointed seats. Those in the pit used the doors in front of them. Stone guided them through the crowds and up the wide stairs to the third floor where they followed others going to their boxes. Stone's was at the end of the corridor and therefore would be close to the stage.

The curtain was opened for them to enter.

The box was empty.

The girls went ahead and were seated at the front of the box.

Amelia hesitated, looking up at the Duke with a frown. 'Where are the rest of your guests?'

He looked surprised. 'The rest?'

'You said you were getting up a party of guests to attend the theatre.'

'You are my only guests.'

A cold feeling settled in the pit of Amelia's stomach. Then he must soon make an offer to Charity. Every member of the *ton* present at the theatre would be expecting it once they saw him alone with her and the Mitchell girls.

Why did dread twist in her chest? She should be thrilled for her protégée. She forced a smile. 'I apologise, Your Grace. I misunderstood.'

'I am Your Grace again, I see. Have I again done something to offend?' He was looking down his nose in that way he had, but there was a glint of amusement in those icy blue eyes.

He was laughing at her?

She felt herself bristle and forced herself to calm. 'Certainly not, Stone. I simply made an incorrect assumption and was surprised.'

He gestured to one of the two remaining chairs at the front of the box. 'Please be seated. May I take your wrap?'

She handed him her shawl and eyed the chair he had indicated. She had expected, as chaperon, to be sitting behind her charges, but now she was being offered a seat in a prime location. She would be able to see the stage perfectly.

A little thrill ran through her. It was an unexpected treat. Everyone knew who she was, what she did to make a living, and while they tolerated her, because of her success, they did not usually treat her as an equal. She smiled up at him. 'Thank you, Stone.'

The expression on his face changed a little, seemed to warm. Or perhaps it was a trick of the light. For in an instant his face was its usual cool, remote, blank slate.

He was a man who did not want anyone to know what he was thinking, least of all a paid employee. Did he ever relax?

Handing him her shawl, she slid into the seat he had indicated, allowing him to sit between her and Charity. Indeed, from this angle she could not see Charity or Patience. Perhaps that was his plan. With her view obstructed…

Good heavens, what was she thinking? The Duke was far to honourable and strait-laced to do anything underhanded.

She settled into her seat and glanced down at the stage. If she was sensible, she would enjoy this evening to the full, because this was likely the last time she would attend the theatre. Once these two young ladies were married off, she was going to retire from the matchmaking business.

The settlements the Duke would make on Charity along with those of her father would provide Amelia with enough of a nest egg that she would be able to live off her investments for the rest of her days.

A little pang of sorrow filled her.

Regret? For what? Not because the Duke would marry Charity. It was not possible. It must be because she had enjoyed helping young people find perfect partners. Every match she had made had proved to be successful both financially and in bringing together two people who fit well together.

She wished she felt the same about Charity and the Duke. They both deserved to be comfortable.

One thing she was sure of—the Duke would never treat Charity badly, even if he was never truly warm to her. He certainly would not gamble his fortune away on horses.

Jasper settled into his seat beside Mrs Durant, puzzled by her reaction to the lack of other guests, but he had also seen the expression of pleasure on her face when she had realised she was to be seated in the best seat in his box.

He could not help but wonder what her life had been like since her come out. He knew of her husband. A man who had insisted on racing his own horse at Newmarket and then broke his neck yards before he was to cross the finishing line first definitely created a memorable impression, even if it was not a good one.

Durant had been from a reasonably good family and there should have been settlements for his widow, but if there had been, she surely would not need to hire herself out.

While she was not being paid as a chaperon, she was certainly being paid to broker matches among the *ton's* younger generation.

Or between heiresses and titles. Like him. While the financial health of the duchy did not necessitate he marry an heiress, if the bride he chose came with a fortune, it was all to the good. On the other hand, he really was free to choose where he pleased, provided he did not tarnish the family name.

He glanced at the beautiful heiresses who were whispering to each other and gazing around them in awe. They were lovely girls, with nice manners and lively dispositions. Either of them would make an excellent wife.

'Is this your first visit to the theatre, Miss Mitchell?' he asked.

Charity turned her limpid blue gaze to meet his. 'I have been to the theatre in York, but of course everything in London is larger, grander and more modern.'

The theatre didn't look particularly modern to him. 'How so?'

'It is much larger than the house in York and the decorations are impressive, do you not think?'

Heavy carvings and lavish gilt were not his favourite.

'And this gas lighting is much brighter than anything I am used to,' she added.

'I have to say the gas lighting is a huge improvement,' he agreed. 'Not only is it brighter, it is not nearly as smoky as oil or candles.'

'Indeed. Or so hot. Mr Dobson says that soon everyone in the country will be using gas to light their homes,' Patience announced.

An enormous undertaking. 'Mr Dobson is likely right.'

He frowned. Wasn't that something the elder Lord Dobson had been also talking about when he had been speaking of an interesting investment.

He really must have his man of business set up a meeting with that gentleman.

He was aware of Mrs Durant listening intently to the conversation between him and the sisters, but she did not participate. It was as if she was distancing herself from the three of them—as a good chaperon should. He did not like it. He wanted to hear her opinion.

'What do you think, Mrs Durant?'

An expression of surprise crossed her face. 'I agree, the gas lighting is not only brighter, but I believe it is safer. At least that is what I have heard. Too many theatres have been lost to fires over the years.

'Yes, indeed.'

The curtains opened and the play began. *Macbeth* was always a favourite with the London audience. Jasper had seen it many times, but he was pleased to discover that the ladies, rather than chattering and giggling through the performance, watched and listened. Of course, that did not mean that the rest of the audience was as well behaved, but his box isolated them from the worst of the riff-raff and, since they were well above the pit, the distractions were minimal.

At intermission, Stone sent one of the footmen to fetch refreshments.

'Oh, look,' Charity said, leaning forward. 'There is Lord Sherbourn.' She frowned. 'He did not mention he planned to attend the theatre tonight when I spoke with him last evening.'

'I expect he decided to attend at the last moment.' Mrs Durant's voice was soothing, as if she was trying to ease some hurt.

Charity's gaze remained fixed on the young lord as if willing him to look up. He did not do so, he was in deep conversation with a group of other young gentlemen.

After a moment or two, she sat back, looking unhappy. Stone glanced at Mrs Durant and discovered she was watching him, as if seeking his reaction.

'They are simply good friends,' she murmured.

He raised an eyebrow.

'Miss Mitchell and Sherbourn.'

Was she trying to give him some sort of assurance? He shrugged. 'I had noticed that they are often in company together.'

Mrs Durant's lips pressed together as if there was something she wanted to say.

A handsome man dressed in exemplary style gazed up into their box with a beaming smile. He doffed his hat and bowed. Jasper stifled a groan. He'd thought Albert was on a repairing lease in the country.

'Who is that fellow staring up here, Charity?' Patience asked. 'Do you know him?'

Charity shook her head. 'I have never seen him before.'

Jasper glared down at Albert. What the devil did he think he was doing?

'He seems to be waiting for an invitation to join us,' Mrs Durant said.

Albert waved.

Jasper glared at him. 'He is a distant cousin of Lady Warren's. He has been out of town.' Damnation. Albert always turned up at the most inconvenient moments and never with good intention. He probably needed a loan.

'Shouldn't you invite him to join us?' Mrs Durant asked.

'I am sure he does not expect it,' Stone said.

Albert took the hint and with a shake of his head turned his attention elsewhere.

She frowned. 'I am quite certain he did.'

'I do not find his company congenial in the least.'

'I see.'

He winced at the disapproval in her tone. She should be disapproving of Albert. 'He is not good *ton*.'

'And one raised eyebrow from you and he scurried off like a rabbit.'

'The ducal stare. I am told it is quite fierce.'

'Devastatingly so.'

She sounded appalled. Had he given her that look when he met her years ago? It would have been in its infancy at the time. Over the years, he had perfected it. Well, there was not much he could do about the past.

'No doubt I shall receive a visit from him tomorrow,' he said calmly, even though the thought made him writhe inside. He endured the man for Aunt Mary's sake.

A footman entered with a tray of drinks and handed them around. 'There is a gentleman outside wishing to know if he can visit, Your Grace.' The man handed over a calling card.

'Is it Mr Dobson?' Patience asked eagerly.

'It is.' Thank God it was not Albert. 'Show him in, please,' Jasper said.

Dobson entered, followed by Sherbourn. 'Look who I found moping about in the lobby,' Dobson said. He bowed. 'Good evening, ladies. Your Grace.'

'Dobson.' Jasper nodded.

He turned his gaze on the other young man, who stopped staring at Miss Mitchell with a besotted expression on his face to shoot his friend a hard look. 'I was not moping.'

The footman offered them both drinks. Dobson accepted. Sherbourn did not. 'I see you are having a grand time, Miss Mitchell,' he said grimly.

She lifted her chin. 'Exceedingly grand, thank you, Lord Sherbourn.'

The young lord glowered at Jasper.

'For goodness' sake, Sherbourn,' Jasper said. 'Accept a glass of wine. You have imposed on my hospitality, now make use of it.'

The young man flushed. 'Indeed, Your Grace, I cannot think why I let Dobson convince me to join you.'

He turned about sharply and left.

Miss Mitchell's eyes sparkled with anger. She gave a little laugh. 'Well, I declare we are better off without him if he is in such an unpleasant temper.'

'Oh,' Dobson said airily, 'take no notice. Sherbourn is always up in the boughs about something or other. So, Miss Patience, what do you make of the gas lights? I told you they were stupendous, did I not? Father had something to do with their installation.'

'I was telling His Grace I thought them quite remarkable.'

Charity looked as if she would like to follow Lord Sherbourn, the foolish chit.

Another gentleman entered the box. Unannounced. Mrs Durant looked startled. 'Uncle Joshua?' She gave Jasper a helpless glance. 'I had no idea you were also in London. May I introduce you to His Grace, the Duke of Stone? Your Grace, Mr Joshua Trotter.'

She looked as if she expected Jasper to cut the man. Did she think him so insufferably high in the instep? He mentally gave his head a shake. Likely had this man approached him in the street, or arrived in his box in Mrs Durant's absence, he would have done so. Mrs Durant would know this.

Was this her way of giving relatives a step up in the world? Somehow, he did not believe it of Mrs Durant.

She seemed genuinely delighted to see her uncle and ready to defend him against Jasper, too. He could not help but admire her loyalty.

And he certainly liked this relative of hers better than Albert. 'Trotter.' He inclined his head.

Mr Trotter bowed as low as a large paunch would allow. 'Honoured, Your Worship. Indeed, I ham.'

Jasper controlled the urge to chuckle at Trotter's attempt to sound refined, because he knew the man was trying his best to show respect.

Trotter turned to his niece. 'My dear girl, such a delight to see you. It is a long time since me and Queenie had the pleasure of your company.' He turned to Jasper and winked. 'Young people these days do not have the least idea of the pleasure their company gives to senior members of their family.'

He pinched Mrs Durant's cheek and leaned in, speaking in a theatrical whisper. 'Your aunt would love you to visit us again, my girl. Never you fear, you will always find a warm welcome at Maldings.'

Mrs Durant smiled at him and there was such fondness in that smile Jasper felt a strange stab of envy. 'I will, Uncle. Very soon, I think.'

The portly man grinned. 'See that you do. Ah, I see the curtain is about to rise. I shall leave you to enjoy the theatrics.' He bowed and left.

Mr Dobson bid them farewell and followed him out.

Jasper gestured to the footman at the back of the box to clear away the glasses and they all took their seats.

'He seemed an interesting man,' he murmured to Mrs Durant, trying to put her at ease.

'Yes, Your Grace. He is.' She sounded defensive. 'The Trotters are relations on my mother's side of the family and the kindest people in the world. I lived with them for a while when my cousin inherited the title. It seems you are not the only one with odd relatives, though I am happy to acknowledge mine.'

Did she expect him to explain Albert who was neither a relation or kind? The less said about him the better.

Chapter Six

Amelia sighed. No doubt she would be receiving a stiff note from some member of the Linden family on the morrow about her temerity in acknowledging her uncle in public.

She hated the snobbery. Joshua Trotter was an honest man and he and his wife had been exceedingly kind to her when she had lost her parents. Their kindness in welcoming her into their family, the fun and the laughter she had encountered among them had been exactly what she had needed. She regretted her hasty departure from their home on the insistence of her Cousin Linden. They had bribed her with the offer of a come out and then married her off as quickly as possible to Durant. A way of them divesting themselves of a connection to those they considered beneath them.

She pushed the thoughts aside. Soon she would have complete independence from her family and she could visit and speak with whomsoever she pleased.

And she certainly did not care a fig for what Stone thought of her relatives. Not one. He was another man too full of his own consequence to see the worth in others. The sooner he made an offer for Charity, the sooner she could be out of his company and getting on with her future.

A pang struck her in the centre of her chest. What? Did she actually care what Stone thought of her? Well, even if she did, there was nothing she could do about it. To prove it, she would write to Uncle Joshua and arrange a visit the moment the Mitchell girls had received their offers of marriage.

When the play finished and the curtain fell, she realised she had not heard one word of what was said on stage, she had been too busy with her whirling thoughts.

Stone placed her wrap around her shoulders as they prepared to leave the box.

'I have never laughed so hard in my life,' Patience said. 'You did not seem to find any humour in the farce, Mrs Durant.'

Amelia blushed. 'I most certainly did.' Dash it all, was she going to lie? 'Or at least I did, when I saw it before. Quite honestly, I was busy with my own thoughts throughout.'

Stone gave her a sharp glance, but did not comment. He expertly guided them out of the theatre to his waiting carriage and, after a little jostling with the other carriages, they were soon on their way home.

She and Stone sat side by side, facing backwards,

while Charity and Patience sat opposite, as his guests. If they had been seated by order of precedence, it was Patience who should have been seated beside the Duke, but given her youth and single state, Amelia had made very sure that did not happen.

The girls chatted happily about the plays they had seen and Stone interjected his views from time to time, leaving Amelia to listen and marvel at his patience. Not for a moment did it appear as if he found their artless chatter and naive comments a trial.

Even if he wasn't particularly warm, it seemed he would be a respectful and kindly husband. If only Charity was not enamoured of Sherbourn, a young man who was up in the boughs one moment and down in the dumps the next. How could Charity prefer him to Stone? It made no sense.

Likely, once Stone proposed and made his admiration clear, the young woman would forget all about Lord Sherbourn. Amelia hoped.

'Do you return to your own house now, Mrs Durant?'

Amelia was jolted out of her unhappy thoughts by the Duke's low voice.

She glanced out of her window and realised they were almost at the Mitchell town house.

'I do, indeed. Mr Mitchell will send me home in his carriage.'

'There is no sense in turning out another coachman, when mine is already on the road. Allow me to drive you.'

It sounded more like a command than a request. Her shoulders stiffened.

'It is the least I can do,' he added.

Dash it, he was right, of course. Despite that she really did not want to be alone with him, there was nothing improper about it, given that the carriage was closed, she was a widow and a respectable chaperon. Indeed, it would look very odd if he did not make the offer and carry it out. It would be ungentlemanly. 'Thank you.'

The carriage pulled up and Stone delivered the two girls to the front door where the butler and a maid were waiting for them.

They would have to forgo their post-mortem of the evening until the morrow. In the meantime, this was her perfect opportunity to discover Stone's intentions and to point out that it was high time he made them clear to the world. The Season was short and if he did not intend to make Charity an offer, they needed to stop wasting their time on him.

She covered her mouth with her hand at the terrible way those thoughts sounded even to her own ears. Mercenary and cold. Had she really become so jaded?

It was not the way she had decided to undertake these matchmaking affairs when she set out. She had planned that only if she could truly see the couple would deal well with each other would she promote a match. Could Charity settle in well with Stone? Indeed, would Stone be satisfied with such a naive young woman as a duchess?

No doubt he planned to mould her to his way of

thinking and going on. But would that sort of structured life make Charity miserable? Amelia felt doubt deep in her bones.

The carriage door opened and Stone climbed in. He took her hand and urged her towards the forward-facing seat. It was a recognition of her rank she had not expected from him, particularly now he had met the distaff side of her family. The man was full of surprises.

Seating himself opposite, he rapped on the ceiling with his cane and the horses moved off. 'So, what had your thoughts so busy during the play, Amelia?'

She started at the use of her first name. Her heart picked up speed in the oddest way. 'I was thinking about my uncle and how soon I might visit Maldings.'

It wasn't the truth, but she could hardly tell him her thoughts had been full of him.

'He is a worthy man.'

She stared at him surprised he would unbend enough to make such an admission. Perhaps her worries about him and Charity were unfounded. 'I am very fond of him and his family. The Lindens prefer not to acknowledge them.'

Was that his sticking point with Charity?

They had arrived at her little house. Perhaps she ought to make Stone aware of how stern he might appear to a young woman as impressionable as Charity. Give him some guidance. 'Would you like to come in for a cup of tea?'

His gaze widened.

Really? Was he thinking she was about to make

inappropriate advances to him. Well, she might like
to, but that was not her purpose.

'Yes,' he said, in that decisive way he had and
jumped down.

After a quiet word with his coachman, he helped
her out of the carriage and escorted her to her front
door.

As she reached her front door, heat rose up from
her belly. Never before had she invited a man to enter
her little home. But the heat was not at all unpleasant.
Indeed, the flutter in her stomach and the pattering
of her heart made her feel young and almost girlish.

But this was nonsense. They were about to speak
of the Duke and his plans to marry Charity.

She opened her front door.

As instructed, Jasper stepped into the parlour
while Mrs Durant asked the maid who had taken
their coats to bring a tea tray. Rarely did he enter
rooms as small as this. It reminded him of the homes
of tenant farmers he had visited upon occasion, only
without the pervading smell of nearby animals. Indeed, all he could smell in here was the scent worn
by Mrs Durant. A combination of exotic spices he
found intriguing.

Like the woman herself.

Just why had she invited him into her home? To
charm him? Somehow it seemed out of character.

Nevertheless, his blood ran warm through his
veins. There really was no denying the spark of attraction he felt whenever she was nearby.

He glanced around the room as if it could give him some clue to the woman herself. The paucity of knick-knacks and memorabilia surprised him. The only painting on the wall was a landscape by an artist he did not know. It was not a feminine room or even homely. It had a temporary feel to it, as if its occupant had merely alighted here for a brief time.

Much like the feeling he got at Stoneborough, the ducal seat. Dukes used it during their term of office and then passed it on to their successors. Some left more of an impression upon the landscape and buildings than others, but all held it in trust. To him, it had never felt like much of a home.

The rustle of skirts had him swinging around. She had removed her headdress and discarded her shawl, but still looked elegant in her pale grey silk gown. Its narrow skirts complemented her slender figure.

'What a charming little home you have here,' he said.

She pursed her lips as if she did not trust his words. 'It is small, I know, and the location not fashionable, but it suits me for the time being.'

Clearly, she had taken his comment as a criticism. 'It seems ideal.'

'For a woman in my position, you mean.'

Prickly female. There really was no pleasing her. Why was he even trying? 'What was your reason for inviting me to take tea with you, Mrs Durant?'

Her eyes narrowed and she gazed at him intently. 'More to the point, my lord Duke, what is holding you back?'

He stiffened at the hostility in her tone. 'I do not take your meaning.'

She closed her eyes briefly. A sweep of long dark lashes. She really did have the most fascinating almond-shaped eyes and perhaps the longest eyelashes he had ever seen.

'With regard to Miss Mitchell,' she said with an impatient wave of her hand. 'If you have concerns about her station in life, for what purpose do you continue to pay her attention?'

Stunned, he stared at her. 'Are you suggesting my intentions are dishonourable?'

'An invitation to share your box, without other guests present, seems a little nearer the mark than I care for. I must think of her reputation. She is a beautiful girl, and wealthy, but you are not in need of wealth.'

He drew himself up and gave her a look that would shrivel any lesser mortal. Except her. She glared back at him.

'Your assumptions with regard to my character are far from complimentary, Mrs Durant. But let me answer your question. I do not feel I know the young woman well enough to make her an offer. That was my intention in making my invitation for this evening. I assumed your presence and that of her sister was enough to stem unwarranted gossip.'

She deflated a little, gestured for him to take a seat and sat down on the sofa. He sat beside her, rather than take the chair opposite.

She shifted uncomfortably, but said nothing.

Good, he wanted her to feel uncomfortable.

'That was what I told myself when I accepted your invitation,' she said, 'but we attracted a great deal of attention and...'

'I always attract a good deal of attention.'

Her eyes widened. Then she nodded as if accepting the truth of his words.

'You know, Mrs Durant, as you yourself have noted, Miss Mitchell seems far more interested in young Sherbourn than she is in me.'

Pink stained her high cheekbones. 'I—'

The maid entered with the tea tray.

Mrs Durant pressed her lips together and waited until the young woman departed before speaking again. 'As I also observed, Miss Mitchell knows where her duty lies.'

The pit of his stomach fell away in a sickening rush he did not understand. Duty had always been his guide. Duty and honour. Doing the right thing for the dukedom and for England.

He had always assumed that it was the right thing for him, too.

He recalled Aunt Mary's blathering about happiness a few days before and the resultant feeling of restlessness. 'Is that to be her fate, then? Married to a man for duty. What of her happiness?'

A frown met his words. A troubled expression. Did she also have doubts?

Mrs Durant gave a little shake of her head. 'She is young. Impressionable. A man like Sherbourn might well turn her head, in the first instance, but that does not mean he will make her happy. It would certainly not please her papa to—'

She hesitated.

'To throw away the chance of marrying a duke in favour of the heir to a penniless earldom.'

'Wealth is not important. Miss Mitchell's fortune will stand her in good stead whomsoever she marries. Her father will see to that. No, it is not that. Lord Sherbourn is very young. I wonder if he is ready to settle down.'

'Not to mention the money you would lose.'

She leaped to her feet. 'You think I would sacrifice the girl's happiness for money?'

He rose. 'I have no idea what your motives are.'

Her dark eyes flashed. Her hand whipped towards his face.

She would have slapped him, if he had not caught her wrist. Her other hand came up and he caught that, too.

He glared down into her furious face, the gold in her eyes glittering with anger. Her rapid breathing causing her lovely bosom to rise and fall within the skimpy confines of her low-cut bodice. She looked magnificent.

He could not help himself.

He kissed her.

For a brief instant, Amelia froze.

How dared he...?

How soft and gentle his lips were against hers.

How fast her heart beat.

How dizzy and breathless she felt.

His grip around her wrists loosened. She tugged slightly and he released her.

She sighed and slid her arms around his firm torso. She had longed to know his kisses from the moment she saw him again in that ballroom. Not true. The longing had started when she was fresh out of the schoolroom when she had been young and impressionable and had stars in her eyes.

She was older now. Wiser. She knew this moment meant nothing more than a kiss between adults who were irresistibly attracted to each other on some animal level they would both prefer to deny.

But denial had not done her a bit of good. The longing would not go away. So why not enjoy the moment and prove to herself her desire was as ill-founded now as it had been when she had been a girl?

Besides, what harm would it do? He was as yet a bachelor and she was a widow. Did she not deserve a little excitement in her life?

She leaned into him, responding to the light pressure of his lips against hers, moving her mouth against him, sipping at him like a butterfly delicately sips nectar.

He raised his head. His expression as he gazed into her face was that of a man bemused. 'I—'

Fearing an apology, she briefly touched a finger to his lips, before brushing it along the hard bone of his jaw and sliding her hand around the back of his neck, urging his head downwards so she could reach his lovely mouth.

Once more their lips melded. This time, the heat of passion made her bold. She responded to the movement of his mouth over hers by parting her lips. His tongue gently flicked across them, tasting, requesting.

Her husband's kisses had been rare and hasty. He'd resented their marriage. Blamed her for it. And perhaps he'd been right to do so.

This kiss was different. Lingering, sweet, unhurried. A gentle exploration. A sense of urgency built within her. A need to know more. This man who seemed so cool, so distant from everyday worries, heated her blood, fevered her mind until she no longer cared about wrong or right.

And besides, once the Mitchell sisters were safely married off, she would retire to the country as she had planned. There would be no running into the Duke at balls or routs and the *ton* would soon forget she ever existed. So why not sample what this man offered?

Likely she would be as disappointed in him as she had been in her husband, which would see an end to her fascination.

She stepped closer and he widened his stance, bringing her body flush with his, her breasts pushing against his chest. A large warm hand cupped her derrière and held her close.

She wound her arms around his neck and swept her tongue inside his mouth, tasting tooth powder and inhaling his spicy cologne that reminded her of dark forests and misty mornings.

A groan rumbled up from his chest, striking an unexpected answering chord of pleasure deep within her body. She stroked her hands down his back while tasting and tangling her tongue with his. Delicious.

The feel of his broad shoulders and strong back beneath her hands was tantalising. She could not help but wonder how he looked beneath his perfect tailoring.

He lifted his head and gazed down at her. 'Without question you entice me, Mrs Durant. Do you mean to do so, I wonder?'

His directness made her smile. There was an honesty about him that was refreshing. He deserved an honest answer. After all, what was the point of beating about the bush at her time of life. 'I most certainly do. Please call me Amelia.'

He sucked in a breath, as if her words affected him physically. It seemed the attraction did indeed go both ways.

'Your reputation—'

'Is mine to care for, Your Grace.'

He stroked a stray hair back from her face with a touch so light she scarcely felt it. 'Jasper.'

She smiled. 'Jasper it is. In private, of course.'

The heat in his gaze seemed to sear her face. 'Well, Amelia, just how private are we?'

'Completely. My maid left for home the moment she delivered our tea.'

'She does not live in?'

He sounded relieved as well as surprised. Was it her reputation or his that gave him concern? And did she really care.

Seduction had not been on her mind when she invited him for tea, but it now seemed inevitable.

'She goes home to her family every night. She stayed a little later this evening so as to be here when I arrived home.'

'To help prepare you for bed.'

'Indeed. But I told her to go.'

'Then you must permit me to oblige you since I have deprived you of her services.'

Yes, she would like that. She touched the tip of his nose with the tip of her forefinger. 'I am quite capable of readying myself for bed, Jasper.'

'Of that I have not the slightest doubt, my dear. You strike me as a most competent woman. But it would be my very great pleasure to assist.'

'Of that I have no doubt,' she said drily.

He chuckled and she joined him in his laughter.

'Speaking of servants, you ought to send your coachman home.'

He gave her a droll look. 'You are not dealing with a flat, Amelia. When a lady invites me into her home, I know better than to leave my carriage hanging about outside her door. I told him not to wait when we stepped down.'

That he would care about her reputation surprised and pleased her. Although, perhaps it was really his own reputation that he cared for. After all, she was not the sort of lady he would normally pursue. His name had been linked with only diamonds of the first water, or high-flying bits of muslin heretofore.

'I certainly do not consider you a flat, Jasper. But

my intentions were only tea and conversation. Nothing else.'

'Until now.'

'Until now.'

He beamed and kissed her hard, leaving her breathless with the heat of it, before saying, 'I do so love your honesty. Shall we retire to your chamber, so I can complete my appointed task?'

She took his hand. 'My bedchamber is at the back of the house. I warn you, it is exceedingly small.'

Chapter Seven

Jasper felt as excited as a lad on his first intimate adventure, instead of a world-weary man about town, as Amelia led him out of the parlour. He had not been entirely surprised at her invitation or the reason for it. But he had been shocked by his response to her anger. He couldn't quite believe that his usual calm had deserted him in the face of her passion. He'd been equally shocked and delighted when she had kissed him back.

At the end of the small hallway a door opened into a kitchen on the right. She opened the door on the left. The bedroom was indeed very small. As was the bed. The curtains of light blue brocade, matching the counterpane, were closed against the night. A night stand, an escritoire and a straight-backed wooden chair were the only other furnishings.

He eyed the bed with misgiving. Clearly designed for one person, the carved frame looked too dainty and fragile to bear his weight. The idea that he might end up on the floor in a tangle of broken wood and bedlinens did not appeal to his sense of dignity.

She was gazing up at him with a frown of concern. Why was he hesitating? Had he become so enamoured with his image of himself as Duke that he was not prepared to take the risk of looking like a mere man?

He swung her around to face him and kissed her, wooing her lips with his. She tasted of honey and exotic spices and her body seemed to fit comfortably with his, her breasts pressing against his chest and her arms snaking around his neck. His heart pounded in his ears as he plundered the depths of her mouth.

She moaned softly, tangling her tongue with his, stirring his body to life and heating his blood. This was why he had accepted her invitation. This sense of recklessness flowing through his veins. He could not recall a time when he had let go of all reason this way.

As Duke he was mindful that every action had a consequence that could bode good or ill and each must be carefully weighed and measured against honour and duty. Right now, honour and duty could go hang.

The kiss ran its course, leaving them both panting, and he raised his head to gaze down into those remarkable eyes of hers. Her lips curved in a naughty smile he had no trouble reading. An invitation to enjoy. His groin tightened.

Anticipation rocketed through him. But he knew better than to rush things. He grinned. 'I had best be about my duty, then, madam. Hmm, where shall

I start? Hair first, I think.' He realised he had been longing to see the true beauty of those shining dark locks she kept so neatly ordered. Would they be straight or would they fall in a riot of curls about her shoulders? With fingers that shook with the intensity of his desire, he felt around amid the heavy tresses for the pins that held them fast. A great many pins, he discovered.

'There is a forest of them,' he grumbled.

She laughed. 'Not that bad, surely?'

'You have the Forest of Dean in here.'

The pile of pins on the escritoire mounted. Finally, he arrived at the heart of the concoction. One pull and a long coil of hair the colour of a blackbird's wing untwined and snaked to her shoulders. It reached the middle of her back. Two more pins extracted and the last two twists came down. He sifted his fingers through the heavy locks until they hung in soft waves. Lovely ripples of black hair. Soft and silky against his skin. And desperately sensual as hell.

A memory of long brown hair came to mind, from when he was a child, watching his mother's toilette. 'Do you have a brush?'

He pushed the memory aside. He did not like to think of his parents. Their loss still hurt.

She opened a drawer in the night table and took out a silver-backed hairbrush and comb. She set them on the escritoire and sat down. 'It doubles as my dressing table.'

A lady of her consequence should be housed in better conditions than this. Perhaps he owned something better. He froze. What was he thinking? He was not in the market for a mistress. He had decided to look for a wife.

Indeed, he should not be entering into any sort of dalliance, now that he had set his feet on the matrimonial path. The Duke in him did not approve at all.

What of the mere mortal man? Was he more likely to succumb to temptation? Dash it all, why should he not have one night for himself and leave ducal duty at the door?

When she was comfortably seated on the little wooden chair, he gathered her hair so it all fell down her back, then began the task of brushing. Long, slow, smooth strokes from the top of her head to the bottom. She made a low soft sound of appreciation and tipped her head back like a cat seeking pleasure. Or a sensual woman.

Desire rode him hard. His pulse quickened. His body demanded. And all he'd done was brush her hair. He took a swift inward breath. Calming his impatience. Wrestling for control. And winning. Barely.

He leaned forward, swept the hair at her nape aside and touched his lips below her ear.

She gasped and shivered.

'If milady would care to rise,' he murmured softly, 'I will help her undress.'

He was intrigued to see how she flattened a hand on the writing surface for support when she rose unsteadily.

Apparently, he wasn't the only one struggling for

control. His desire notched higher. He quelled his impatience. Good things were worth waiting for.

He pushed her hair over one shoulder and unknotted the lace at the neck of her gown. Gently he eased the strings through the top two holes, revealing the expanse of smooth skin across her shoulders. A dark mole resided beside the second notch of her spine. A beauty spot indeed. He pressed his lips against it. She gave a little moan and tipped her head back, her cheek brushing against his in a whisper of skin against skin.

Once more, he pushed her hair aside and tackled the tapes on her gown, gradually moving downwards, revealing the top of her delicate shift and the sturdy linen of her stays, also laced tightly. It was like unwrapping a particularly precious gift. He resisted the temptation to hurry to the prize. Instead, he lingered over the task, touching and kissing his way down her back inch by inch until both gown and stays were completely open. He eased the gown off her shoulders, down her arms and over her hands. It slid to the floor and puddled at her feet. The stays dropped away, leaving her standing in a veil of sheer muslin, dipping slightly at the waist and clinging to the curves of her lovely derrière.

He shaped her with his hands, learning those delicious curves and hollows. 'Lovely,' he murmured.

She turned in his arms and buried her blushing face against his shoulder. 'Thank you,' she whispered. 'You make me feel beautiful.'

Surprised, he grasped her upper arms and eased her back so he could see her face. 'You are lovely, which is why I do not understand my lack of recollection of our first meeting. Your beauty struck me the moment I saw you at Sally Jersey's ball.'

'We were introduced at Almack's and met again a few days later at a ball.' She stroked his cheek with her fingertips. 'In those days, I was painfully shy and thin, all awkward elbows and frilly dresses that suited me not at all.'

'And no doubt I was a pompous ass. I apologise.'

She rose up on her tiptoes and pressed a swift kiss to his lips. 'There, you are forgiven.'

'Thank you.'

She cast her gaze downwards as if she did not believe him, but a little smile of pleasure curved her lips.

He wanted to assure her that his gratitude was heartfelt, but he did not have the words to do it. But he would show her with his lips and his body and touch. He knelt at her feet.

A little gasp said he had surprised her. He lifted the hem of her chemise with his teeth and untied each little white garter with its blue rosette. He rolled each stocking down to her ankles, while she supported herself with her hands on his shoulders. Her fingers trembled where they gripped him. She lifted a foot and he eased the silky stocking off her long slender foot. He kissed the arch and massaged the sole. She made a sound of pleasure in her throat.

'That is so good,' she murmured. 'My maid certainly does not do that.'

He glanced upwards and grinned. 'So I should hope.' What a delight she was. Her obvious enjoyment of his attentions made him feel extraordinarily pleased with himself. He hadn't felt this way since he was a lad. Before he had picked up the burden of his title.

It was a good feeling. He rose to his feet and lifted her on to the bed, feasting his eyes on the beauty sprawled before him languid and inviting.

At her smile of invitation, he hastily stripped off his clothes. A button off his shirt pinged against the window. She giggled.

He beamed as he pulled it over his head. Her giggle charmed him. He felt like giggling himself.

He toed off his shoes, ripped off his stockings, hesitating for a moment while he glanced at her face. She licked her lips.

He almost groaned out loud. He whipped off his pantaloons and lay close beside her, brushing the hair back from her face. She rolled on her side and wriggled one hand under his neck. The other she placed on his behind and pulled him close.

He kissed her and brought her body flush with his. The heat at her centre almost undid him. He slid a hand down between them and slipped one finger inside her wet heat. She sighed. That sigh went straight to something deep in his heart. A sweet painful welling of some emotion that left him feeling weak. Humbled. This woman undid him on so many levels.

When she urged him to roll on top of her, he complied instantly, gazing down into her face. With her hands about his neck she raised herself up and kissed his lips briefly. 'I want you,' she murmured.

He entered her swiftly, his shaft hardening as he thrust into her and his ballocks drawing up tight. It took all his control not to fall apart in an instant, but to pleasure her as she deserved to be pleasured. He watched her face, the tension, the sound of her sighs and moans urging him on, yet he held back until he saw her eyes open wide, felt her shudder around him.

Hastily he withdrew from her and fell into bliss.

His last conscious thought was to use the corner of the sheet to wipe the mess from her lovely belly.

Amelia, bolstered by pillows and feeling an unusual sense of well-being, sipped at the hot chocolate her maid had brought in a few moments before. It was always her favourite part of the day. A time for quiet reflection.

Last night had been the most exciting, delicious experience of her life. That she had not expected.

What a fool she had been to think that bedding the Duke would deal with her unwanted infatuation. He had been a wonderfully tender and skilled lover. Now she wanted him more than ever.

And he wanted to see her again.

Her heart gave an odd little jolt, painful and sweet at one and the same time. This was wrong.

She was supposed to be arranging a match between him and Charity. She stared down into her cup. On the other hand, Charity would be perfectly happy with Lord Sherbourn. More than happy.

Even Jasper, a man she had thought so full of his own consequence he expected all to worship at his feet, had noticed Charity was more interested in her young suitor than she was in a duke. Amelia could not understand Charity's thinking when Jasper was not only the most sought-after bachelor in the country, but also a much better man than the sulky, moody Lord Sherbourn. Still, if Charity could not see it, why try to make her see sense?

Pain stabbed at her heart. Amelia sat upright and put her cup aside. What on earth was she thinking? That Jasper would marry her instead of Charity? Last night was not the behaviour of a prospective suitor. The Duke wasn't courting her. He had made her his lover. He'd crept out of her bed and her house at three in the morning because he didn't want anyone linking their names—any more than she did.

When he chose a bride, it would either be the beautiful Miss Mitchell or it would be someone from the upper echelons of the *ton*. She could think of at least three young ladies making their debut this Season who would fit the bill.

A widow who needed to make her living by making matches among the members of the *ton* was fair game as a mistress, but not marriage material.

Besides, she did not want to be married. Her first experience as a wife had been completely unsatisfactory. Her husband had resented being trapped into marrying her, even though he had been the one to steal an illicit kiss. Once they were wed he had refused to listen to any of her opinions, never heeded her advice on any issue. He'd done exactly as he pleased because men could and there was nothing any wife could do about it.

She sighed and shook her head at herself. She'd made it easy for Durant. She'd behaved like a fool, dancing and flirting with the first man to show her any attention, proving to herself she did not care that the Duke had as good as given her the cut direct.

Recalling her youthful misbehaviour made her go hot and cold all over. Without doubt, her bold manner had given Durant the wrong impression of her character.

How naive she had been when he offered to show her the orangery. At the start, there had been four of them trekking across the lawn to the glasshouse at one side of the house. In hindsight, she had realised that he had planned for his friend to leave them alone among the trees to explore more than the plants.

Unfortunately for him, her aunt had spotted them leaving the ballroom and, along with her cousin and his wife, had followed them, intending to bring her back. Her family had arrived to find Durant pressing her against a wall and with his tongue in her mouth and one hand on her breast.

It didn't matter that she was trying to fight him off. She was ruined.

If it had been only her family who had witnessed the shocking kiss, she might have escaped unscathed, but the mass exodus of the Linden party had attracted the notice of the biggest scandalmonger in London who had tagged along. The news of her shocking behaviour had travelled among the rest of the assembled company like wild fire.

Durant had found himself leg-shackled within the week. Something he had made her regret for the rest of their married life, which had not been that long, a mere two years, though it had seemed like an eternity at the time. When Durant died, she had sworn she would never let herself be fooled by any man again.

And now she was treading the same path with Jasper, only this time she had become what she had always scorned, a wanton widow.

And it had been wonderful.

And he wanted to meet her again.

Her stomach fluttered. A masked ball at Vauxhall sounded deliciously exciting and wicked. And why not? It wasn't as if he had offered for Charity yet. If he declared himself—when he did, she corrected herself—then their affair would end. It must. She would never come between a betrothed couple. And never between husband and wife. But in the meantime… She stretched, luxuriating in the feel of a body well loved—yes, until then what harm could it do?

They were both adults. They both understood the rules of the game. As long as she did not let her heart rule her head, all would be fine.

She rang the bell for her maid. She needed to bathe before dressing and starting her day. And then she must find a suitable costume to wear to the ball. Something that would hide her identity. She did not have much time.

A trickle of something hot ran through her veins. The thought of seeing Jasper again.

It seemed that after all this time, after discovering just how wonderful a man could be as a lover, she could not resist his allure. It was going to take more than one night of lovemaking to cure her infatuation.

Jasper regarded himself in the mirror. With a false moustache, a black velvet mask, a tricorne hat and a frock coat fashionable in the previous century, he hardly recognised himself. Not that his disguise could be deemed extraordinary. Likely he would not be the only highwayman at the ball. No, what made him feel like someone else altogether was that he was actually contemplating attending a masked ball. He'd always viewed them as an excuse for sensible people to act out of character. A duke did not do that sort of thing.

It was beneath his dignity.

He could not wait. Which was why he did not recognise himself. There was a sense of excitement within him he did not recall ever feeling before. A restlessness. Or perhaps he did recall it. Somewhat. In the years before his parents died, he'd felt similar feelings at Christmas and birthdays, had he not? But those were childish feelings, put aside when he had become Duke at the ripe old age of fifteen. The responsibilities of the dukedom had rested heavily upon his shoulders since then. Aunt Mary had made very certain he knew exactly what was required of him and had guided him along a strict path. What would

Aunt Mary think of him now? Would she recognise him as the dutiful Duke she had raised?

Would he recognise Amelia? Of course, he would. Whatever disguise she had chosen to wear, he would know her by the exotic shape of her eyes and the tilt of her chin.

More to the point, would she recognise him? He turned this way and that and winced. Perhaps he should not have let his beard grow for the past two days. It now looked quite scruffy, when he was always meticulously clean shaven.

He should have sent her a note describing his costume. He glanced at the clock. Too late now. He had arranged to meet her there at eleven and she must be on her way. He strode downstairs and out of the house. Normally he would have called for his carriage. Tonight, however, he was travelling incognito.

The night was pleasantly warm, the air clear, since few fires would have been lit on such a fine evening, and the summer was not far enough along for the heat to cause the river to stink. It would not be long, however, before London became unpleasantly smelly and the members of the *ton* returned to their homes in the country.

As he drew nearer to the ferry that would take him across the river, he had the odd sensation he might be making a terrible mistake. His suggestion that they meet at Vauxhall had been pure spur of the moment. He'd feel like a fool if she did not show up. If so, he would slip quietly away.

Indeed, it would be better if she did not show up. Would it not? He could then go back to being himself.

He took a deep breath, relaxed his shoulders and sauntered down the steps to the river. On the other side, he joined a group of rowdy young gentlemen as they made their way along the walks to the centre of the gardens where boxes surrounded the dance floor. Men and women in costumes ranging from gauzily clad female nymphs to a man wearing a moth-eaten bearskin milled about with drinks. At one end an orchestra played a waltz and shepherdesses and Roman senators whirled about the space set aside for dancing.

Oddly, only one woman really caught his attention. She was dressed in a full-skirted gown with the sides drawn up to reveal her petticoat, carrying a basket of oranges and wearing a sequin-covered mask over the upper portion of her face. She was the right height and when she turned to scan the crowds around him, he knew he had found his Amelia.

His? His for tonight, at least. For she would not have come here if he had not asked her to attend. Of that he was certain. Before he could reach her another gentleman dressed as a pirate had reached her side, bowing and clearly asking her to dance. At any other sort of dance, he would simply have indicated his prior claim to the lady and the other man would have withdrawn. Tonight, he intended to keep his rank hidden and enjoy himself as if he was an ordinary man.

But it certainly had its disadvantages.

She hesitated, then shook her head.

Relief flooded through him. Clearly, she had recognised that this man was not whom she sought. He strolled to her side. 'Good evening, my lady,' he said softly.

She glanced up at him and he was surprised to see worry in her eyes. Then she must have recognised him because the worry fled and she smile. 'Your—'

He touched a finger to her lips. 'Tonight, I am simply Dick Turpin. And you, I am guessing from your orange basket, are Nell Gwyn?'

'It was all I could think of at the last moment and the costume was easy enough.'

'It suits you.'

She frowned.

Damn, he had meant it as a compliment, but he could see she did not see it that way. 'You look lovely.'

'Thank you.' She smiled and there was a shyness to it he had not expected. It was as if their disguises made them two different people.

His heart felt strangely large as if it was overflowing with an emotion he did not understand. The orchestra began another waltz. 'May I request your hand for this dance?'

'With pleasure.'

He swept her on to the floor. She felt so good in his arms, so right, that he could only kick himself for not having recognised her beauty the first time they met. Likely it was not long after his disastrous attempt to find romance where none existed, when he'd realised people cared nothing for the man beneath the title of Duke and he'd distanced himself from society at large.

Aunt Mary had drilled him by the hour until he knew the name of every nobleman in the country. He had met many of their daughters, but had avoided all women like the plague, in case one of them tried to trap him into marriage.

Now, he knew better than to fear matchmaking mothers. The Duke of Stone would not be bullied. He was high enough in status to be a law unto himself. Not that he would ever take advantage of a woman because of it. He had been brought up to be an honourable man.

For the most part.

It was not exactly honourable to lure Amelia Durant to an event such as this. And yet, for once, he was filled with the need to be reckless. He glanced down at his partner. 'May I be honest?'

Her eyes widened in surprise, but she nodded. 'I would prefer it if you were.'

Yes, and he liked her because of it. 'This is the first time I have ever attended a Vauxhall Masquerade. I have been to a few private parties masked, of course, but never one open to the public as this one is.'

She nodded as if she was not at all surprised. And, strangely, that troubled him.

'This is my first time at Vauxhall Gardens,' she admitted, 'though I have heard a great deal about it over the years.'

'You did not come here during your come out?'

'No. My Season was very short. I married within a month of my arrival in London.'

He was not at all surprised that an exotic flower such as she would have been snapped up right away.

He glanced around as they circled the floor. Even though the evening was early, several of the young dandies in attendance were visibly inebriated. 'It is not usually so rackety. Masks seem to give people the idea that they can do anything they want without consequence.'

He frowned as a young woman leaned out of one of the boxes to help drag a fellow over the railing and into her box where she proceeded to kiss him soundly. Another man was dancing far too close to his partner, whose gown was shockingly revealing. These events attracted not only the *ton*, but the demimonde also. One thing was certain, he was not going to leave Amelia's side for a second.

'Are the walks as dark as they say, I wonder?' she said, watching a young man lead his partner down one of the paths that ended up here in the centre of the gardens. 'The pathway I followed from the entrance was well lit, I noticed.'

'As most of them are. What are called the dark walks are at the periphery of the gardens. Not the place for a lady. But come, let us explore a little before we have supper.'

The dance finished and he led her away from the music and the crowds, taking a path lit by lanterns strategically suspended in trees. They walked arm in arm and they viewed the grottos, where statues and bushes were artfully lit from beneath. They wandered through a brightly lit maze. He admired the waterwheel, the fountains and other features of the gardens until they reached the end of the strings of lights and the path disappeared into the gloom. All around them could be heard giggles and whispered conversations.

Unable to resist, he pulled her into a nearby alcove cut into a yew bush and tipped her face up to his with one finger. He waited a moment. Gave her a chance to protest.

When she did not, he pulled her close and kissed her. Instantly, she twined her arms about his neck and kissed him back. His heartbeat sounded loud in his ears and drummed in his chest. His blood ran hot. He stroked her back and she made a soft sound of longing in the back of her throat.

His body responded to the sound, hardening, desiring.

And this was why a gentleman did not take a lady into the dark walks of Vauxhall.

He broke the kiss and took a deep breath.

Even in the shadowy dark, he could see she was smiling.

'You lead me astray, madam,' he said, trying to control his breathing.

She laughed outright. 'Sirrah, it is you who dragged me into the bushes.'

'If I was to drag you into the bushes, you would not be laughing.'

She placed a hand flat on his shoulder. 'No, indeed, I would not. And I trust you would not do such a thing or I would not have let you lead me here.'

Trust. To have earned it from her made his heart

swell. He cupped her face in his hands. 'You deserve much better than a quick tumble in the dark walks of Vauxhall, my dear. Come. Our supper is ordered. You will give me your opinion on the shaved ham. It is touted by all as their speciality.'

He put an arm about her waist and she rested her head against his upper arm as they walked back the way they had come.

As they crossed the brightly lit dance floor, a gentleman in medieval garb, with the cowl of his costume making it impossible to see his face, almost collided with Jasper.

'Look where you are going, why don't you?' he snapped.

'I might say the same to you,' Jasper said coldly.

'Good Lord! Coz, is it really you?'

Jasper stiffened. 'Albert?'

The man chortled. 'Of all people, you are the last I would expect to bump into at Vauxhall. Well met.' He peered at Amelia. 'And who is this lovely? Not Mrs Garnet. Well, well. Are you going to introduce me?'

'Albert Carling, meet Nell Gwyn,' he said haughtily.

'You old dog!' Albert exclaimed. 'Mum's the word.' He bowed. 'I wish you a pleasant evening.'

He hurried off.

'Damn,' Jasper muttered. 'Of all the people to run into us, it would have to be him.'

'You do not want it bruited about that the Duke of Stone attended such a boisterous affair, no doubt.' She sounded cool and kept her face averted.

'I do not want people trying to guess the name of the lady the Duke of Stone brought to Vauxhall.'

'Naturally,' she said, but the idea did not seem to please her.

'Amelia, are you telling me you wish to have it known by all and sundry you are here cavorting with me? For, be assured, Albert Carling would be only too happy to dine out on that titbit for a month.'

Her lovely mouth drooped for a second and then she smiled, but it looked a little forced. 'You are right, Jasper. It would not do at all.'

Damn. He should never have come here. It was just the sort of place he could expect to run into Albert.

He guided her into the box and signalled to a waiter, who immediately brought them a bottle of champagne and two glasses.

'Your supper will be served shortly, Mr Smith,' the waiter said.

Amelia stared at him in surprise. 'Mr Smith?'

'We are incognito, are we not?'

After a moment's hesitation, she raised her champagne glass in a toast. 'Here is to our evening at Vauxhall.'

Why did he sense an air of sadness in her? But, no, her eyes were sparkling and her lips curved in a happy smile. He was imagining it. This evening was as perfect as he had planned and he was looking forward to taking her home.

'To our evening at Vauxhall,' he replied, lifting his glass in return. 'I am so glad to have the pleasure of your company.'

She started, her lovely mouth forming an 'o' of surprise. 'Jasper, that is the loveliest thing anyone has ever said to me.'

Anyone? Surely…

Supper arrived and was laid out between them on a small table. They shared the shaved ham and buttered crusty bread along with a lobster and thinly sliced cucumber.

'The ham lives up to its reputation,' Amelia said. 'And the wine is delicious.'

He poured her another glass. 'Then we must not let it go to waste.'

A young fellow dressed as a Roman in a toga made from a bedsheet and slung carelessly over his shoulder leaned into their box.

'Pretty, witty Nell Gwyn, will you grant me this next waltz?'

The brandy on his breath wafted into the box and Amelia drew back from his groping hand.

'The lady is not interested,' Jasper said coldly.

'Can she not speak for herself?' the unruly fellow asked, with a leer.

'I most certainly can,' Amelia said. 'While you may be able to quote the great diarist himself, your behaviour is not gentlemanly, sir, and I would be obliged if you would depart immediately.'

Pride filled Jasper at her lack of fear. 'You heard the lady.'

Chapter Eight

⤜⤛⤜⤛

Amelia was beginning to think this little adventure of hers was more than she could handle. First an uncomfortable meeting with Jasper's cousin and now the belligerent young man who would not leave.

When Jasper rose to his feet, looking every inch a duke, at least in Amelia's eyes, the young man muttered an unpleasant curse and backed away.

She frowned. 'Jasper, do you know that young man?'

Jasper shook his head. 'He is no acquaintance of mine? Do you recognise him?'

She watched him retreat around the dance floor. Her stomach sank. 'Oh, dear. I remember now. He is one of Lord Sherbourn's set. A Mr Cox. And, if I am not mistaken, the person he is talking to, the one dressed in an artist's smock and wearing a beret, is Lord Sherbourn. Dash it. They are looking this way. Mr Cox must have recognised one or other of us.'

'Are you certain it is Sherbourn? He looks quite the card in that get up.'

She stifled a laugh. He did look very foolish, though no doubt he thought himself quite the romantic. 'I would recognise that cleft in his chin anywhere.'

But being recognised by Lord Sherbourn wasn't the worst of it. A sylph-like young woman in the costume of a fairy queen hung on his arm. A costume Amelia had heard described more than once. 'Oh, no! It cannot be.'

'Cannot be what?' Jasper said, his gaze narrowing.

'The young fool.'

'Who are you talking about?' Jasper asked. 'Sherbourn?'

'No. Charity. She is also here.'

The ducal expression of disapproval settled on his face. 'I see.'

What did he see? Dash it. How like a man. It was all very well for him to go to Vauxhall with a woman he did not intend to wed, but it was not all right for his intended to follow in his footsteps. On the other hand... 'If her papa ever finds out—I need to take her home.'

Jasper sighed. 'Let me handle this, my dear, since you will not wish her to know you are here with me.'

Her stomach dipped. He was right. 'Oh, dear, this is dreadful.'

He glared at the party on the other side of the dance floor. 'Not nearly as dreadful as young Sherbourn risking her reputation. Wait here.'

'No. It will not do. What if someone has already

guessed at her identity? We must make it clear to all and sundry that she is here with a proper chaperon and as the guest of the Duke of Stone. There is no other choice.'

He made a sound of impatience. 'I would far rather teach Sherbourn a lesson. What is he thinking, risking her reputation that way? Not to mention yours.'

'Mine?' She laughed and it sounded brittle. 'How is mine at risk?'

'You may not have noticed, but several of those present have been wondering who it is who has come on the Duke of Stone's arm. They know we arrived together and dined alone. Once they put two and two together, the whole evening will be turned into a scandal broth.'

'My reputation matters not a whit since I am not in the market for a husband and you cannot mean to throw Charity to the wolves, surely? No one will give you the lie if you say we are a party of four that got split up earlier in the evening.'

He grimaced. 'Very well, but try not to look so anxious and we will see what we can do to carry this off.'

He was right. She schooled her face into calm cheerfulness. 'Let us go.'

They reached the group in short order. They seemed to be in the middle of an argument and ceased their discussion at Amelia and Jasper's approach.

Jasper bowed and at that moment looked the very epitome of a rakish highwayman. 'Miss Mitchell.

Sherbourn. At last we find you. We quite lost sight of you in this crowd.'

Charity's mouth dropped open.

Sherbourn stuck out a belligerent jaw. 'Stone. What do you want? You and your bit of muslin aren't welcome.'

Amelia gasped.

'You will keep a civil tongue in your head, you idiot,' Jasper growled. 'Mrs Durant and I are here to save you from your folly.'

'Mrs Durant?' Charity exclaimed. 'I am so glad to see you. I have never felt so uncomfortable in my whole life.' She sounded closes to tears. 'I should never have come.'

'No, you should not have,' Jasper said harshly.

'Now, now,' Amelia said, not wanting to start the girl off sobbing. 'It is a mistake to be sure, but as long as you are properly chaperoned, there is no harm done.'

Charity turned on her co-conspirator. 'You said it was perfectly respectable as long as no one recognised me, but that man—' She shuddered.

'What man?' Jasper said, sounding menacing.

'You have no need to worry about him,' Sherbourn said stiffly. 'I sent him to the right about, I can tell you.'

'Miss Mitchell should not have been exposed to such insult,' Jasper replied equally stiffly.

Oh, dear, it seemed they might be about to come to fisticuffs over Charity's honour. Amelia had not realised the Duke felt so strongly.

Charity sniffled. 'Lord Sherbourn threatened to run him through.'

Just the sort of thing that would get them noticed. 'Charity, do not weep. You will draw attention to us all,' Amelia said sternly. 'Let us return to the Duke's box where we can observe the festivities in private.'

'You have a box?' Charity's eyes widened. 'Lord Sherbourn said they were dreadfully expensive.'

Sherbourn bristled at this roundabout criticism of his arrangements for the evening.

'Never mind that,' Amelia said hastily. She took Charity's arm and walked her back to the box, smiling and talking trivialities as if nothing was wrong. She was grateful when a servant opened the door and they tucked themselves into its shadowed privacy. She let go a sigh of relief.

'Oh…' Charity sighed '…this is most comfortable. Mrs Durant, do look at that woman in the flowing red gown. I swear she has dampened her petticoats. Who is she supposed to be, do you think?'

Lord Sherbourn glowered. 'Not the sort of woman you should be emulating.'

'It might have been better if you had thought of that before you brought her,' Jasper muttered.

'I didn't know she was going to appear in such a scanty get up,' Sherbourn replied. 'She said she had something she had worn to a ball in York. Something her papa had approved of, therefore I assumed it would be perfectly respectable.'

'It is perfectly respectable,' Charity flashed back. 'You are such a prude.'

This must be the reason for the argument she and Jasper had interrupted. 'Do you have a cloak, Charity?'

'Oh, yes,' Charity said. She winced. 'I left it on the chair where we were sitting.'

'I will fetch it,' Jasper said.

'No,' Sherbourn said. 'I should have remembered it. I will get it.'

'Let me go, Sher,' his friend said. 'I'll be back in a trice.' He escaped as if the devil was after him. Clearly, he was not enjoying the atmosphere in the box.

'Have you had supper?' Amelia asked.

'I was about to order it, when you and the Duke showed up,' Sherbourn said. 'As soon as a table came free.'

Jasper heaved a long-suffering sigh and beckoned a waiter to attend them.

Amelia felt like heaving a sigh herself. For a time, being here with Jasper had been like a girlish dream come true. Finding Charity here was like divine retribution for something she should never have embarked on. An affair with the Duke of Stone. The suitor of one of her clients. If she was careful, Charity might never realise she and the Duke had chosen Vauxhall for an assignation. But it must never happen again.

'Does Patience know you are here?' she asked.

'No,' Charity murmured, looking shamefaced. 'She would have been sure to talk me out of it. And I so wanted to see the fireworks. I love fireworks.'

Amelia had also wanted to see the fireworks.

She glanced around. Were people looking at them? She could not tell. Jasper was right, though, there had been one or two curious glances sent their way when they were dancing. This evening had all the makings of a disaster.

Mr Cox came up to the front of their box and handed Charity's cloak to Sherbourn. 'If you will excuse me,' the young man said with a wary glance at Jasper, 'I have seen a friend of mine and I think I will join him.' He gave his friend an anxious glance. 'I think it would be best if I do not mention that Miss Mitchell came with me and Sherbourn.'

Charity beamed. 'Thank you, Mr Cox.'

'On the contrary,' Jasper said sternly. 'You will tell your friend that you met Miss Mitchell and that she is a member of the Duke of Stone's party.'

Cox looked puzzled.

Sherbourn looked bitter.

Amelia smiled at the young man. 'It is the truth, is it not? Here we all are, in the Duke's box.'

Cox looked at Sherbourn, who nodded, albeit a little unwillingly. Cox's brow cleared. 'Sher, I told you it was not a good idea to bring a debutante to Vauxhall without her papa's permission. This will serve. Indeed, it will.' He bowed and left.

Jasper leaned close and murmured in Amelia's ear, 'It seems Sherbourn's friend has a smidgeon of sense, even if it is after the fact.'

Yes, and if they wanted the gossips to accept their story they would have to act as if it was the truth. 'I believe we should stay for the fireworks. Would it not look odd if we left before the highlight of the evening?'

For a long moment Jasper gazed at Charity. Was he displeased at her attendance here with Sherbourn? Displeased enough to wash his hands of her? Perhaps he saw the entreaty in Charity's expression and found himself unable to resist her appeal, because he nodded. 'Very well. We will stay for the fireworks.'

Charity clapped her hands. 'Thank you, Stone.'

He gave her an indulgent smile.

Amelia's heart gave a painful squeeze.

This was not the evening Jasper has intended. But Amelia was right, they had to act as if all was well. Why on earth had he got himself tangled up in such a farce in the first place? Because he had wanted to spend time with Amelia, the way any ordinary man would.

What a ridiculous idea.

The moment they'd arrived he'd been recognised. There was no way Miss Mitchell's identity would remain a secret either. The only one way to rescue her reputation was to act as if he had indeed invited her and her chaperon, along with the sulky Sherbourn to the masquerade.

His name and Miss Mitchell's would be on everyone's tongue by morning.

Exactly as Amelia hoped, no doubt.

He glanced at the matchmaker. Yes, she was looking very pleased with herself. Had she planned this? She had been very quick to suggest that he rescue the fair damsel in distress. He sipped at his champagne and observed the beautiful Miss Mitchell. Would he be happy married to such an innocent?

She would be putty in his hands, easily moulded into the sort of wife any man would want on his arm. But would he be happy? There was that word again. It seemed to have lodged in his brain when he thought he had excised it years ago.

Sherbourn ate little of the second supper Jasper ordered. Naturally, nor did Amelia. But Miss Mitchell set about hers with gusto, exclaiming over the deliciousness of every bite. When she was done, Jasper waved over their waiter and had him remove the dishes.

The orchestra struck up another tune and Miss Mitchell tapped her foot in time to the music.

'Would you care to dance, Miss Mitchell?' Jasper asked. For the sake of appearances, it was the right thing to do at this juncture.

'I would love to,' Miss Mitchell responded. 'But they have played nothing but waltzes all evening.'

'Miss Mitchell does not waltz,' Sherbourn said repressively.

'I think you should waltz with the Duke,' Amelia said brightly. 'After all, you do have permission and I had intended you should at the next assembly we attended.'

'May I indeed?' Miss Mitchell said. She jumped to her feet and kissed Amelia on the cheek. 'Oh, wait until I tell Patience. She will be so jealous.'

Stone and Sherbourn rose with her.

'You may,' Amelia said 'But you will observe the proper distance and only dance once.'

'Her first waltz should be with me,' Sherbourn muttered. 'I brought her.'

'Without permission,' Amelia said severely.

Sherbourn glowered at Charity. 'Do you want to waltz with Stone?'

She looked stricken. 'I— Do you not want me to?'

Sherbourn brushed back a lock of hair from his forehead. 'You must do as you please.' He leaped over the box railing and strode away.

Miss Mitchell went bright pink.

Jasper sighed. Sherbourn was such an idiot.

'Yes, Stone,' Miss Mitchell said with a toss of her head. 'I will waltz with you.'

He took her arm and led her out on to the dance floor.

Amelia thought the evening would never end. When Charity returned to their box after her dance with Jasper, she seemed in excellent spirits, whereas Amelia felt empty.

Having already decided this would be her last meeting with Jasper, she had hoped it would be memorable. Now it was a memory that would be tarnished. She carefully seated herself a little apart from the couple, making it clear she was merely the chaperon. By tomorrow, all would know the Duke was about to make an offer for Miss Mitchell and the *ton* would expect to hear a betrothal was in the offing.

It was what she had hoped for from the beginning.

At last she would be able to buy her little house in the country and retire to enjoy her gardening and the quiet social life a country village could offer a widow.

As if to show her willingness to fall in with these plans, Charity kept up a stream of artless chatter to which Jasper—His Grace—responded by nodding indulgently while he sipped his wine until groups of people began to leave the rotunda and make their way towards the open area where the fireworks could be seen to their best advantage.

'Shall we go see the fireworks?' Stone asked rising from his seat.

'Oh, yes,' Charity said. 'Do you think we can acquire a place near the front, so I can see everything?'

'I have no doubt His Grace can manage that,' Amelia said.

The Duke gave her a sharp glance, but said nothing. Having escorted them out of the box, he linked his arm with Charity and then held his other arm out to Amelia. Not to take it would have seemed rude. She hooked her arm through his.

They followed the general exodus and, exactly as she expected, he found them the perfect spot from which to observe the fireworks, unobstructed.

The fireworks showering light overhead were beautiful, but they were not the pièce de résistance. It was the set pieces that were astonishing in their complexity. A carriage and horses looked as if it was moving, a waterfall that tumbled into a pool and, the grand finale, words of farewell that seemed to move across the sky.

At the conclusion, Charity clapped her hands. 'Bravo. I have never seen the equal of that. Thank you, Stone.'

'You are welcome, Miss Mitchell.' He turned to Amelia. 'I hope you found them equally entertaining, Mrs Durant?'

She had been feeling too disappointed to really enjoy them. 'I did indeed, Stone. Most enjoyable.'

She had tried to sound enthusiastic, she really had, but from the tightening of Jasper's lips and his frown, she had failed miserably. Yet there was no denying that the fireworks had been splendid.

'It is time I got you ladies home,' Jasper said.

Amelia had the feeling he could not wait to be rid of them. A thought that made her heart feel truly heavy. Tonight, they had cast the die. He would have no option but to offer for Charity. She forced her lips to smile. 'Indeed. Let us go before it becomes too difficult to find a ferry to take us across.'

'No need,' Jasper said. 'My carriage is now waiting upon the road yonder. I will have us back across the bridge in no time at all.'

As he had predicted, they were among the first to leave and they crossed London Bridge in short order. At the Mitchell residence, Amelia climbed out with Charity.

'May I drop you at your house, Mrs Durant?' Jasper asked.

While she was tempted to say yes, Amelia shook her head. 'I have a room here for the night. Mr Mitchell arranged it for the nights when we are late home from a ball or a party. I shall make use of it this evening.'

'Thank goodness,' Miss Mitchell said. 'For I see a light in Papa's study and I fear he knows I went out and will demand an explanation.'

Jasper looked at her. 'Do you wish me to come in with you?'

'That will not be necessary,' Amelia said. 'Do not worry, Charity, I will make everything right with your papa. Goodnight, Stone. Thank you for a pleasant evening.'

Jasper saw them to the door and gave them both a hard smile. 'Goodnight, ladies.'

The butler let them in.

Chapter Nine

The next day, Aunt Mary interrupted Jasper's meeting with his man of business.

'I beg your pardon,' she said. 'I did not realise you were busy.'

Well, that was a bouncer. Aunt Mary always knew exactly what was going on.

'I think we have completed our business, have we not, Trim?'

'Yes, Your Grace. Nothing else that cannot wait.' His man of business bowed himself out and Aunt Mary took his seat in front of Jasper's desk.

'What are your intentions with regard to Miss Mitchell?'

Another woman asking him the question.

'Do you also think I should make her an offer?' he asked lazily.

His aunt shot him a look. 'Do not use that tone with me, Jasper. I am not deceived. You are annoyed at my asking.'

He picked up his pen and ran the quill though his fingers. 'Then why do it?'

'Naturally, I think only of your happiness.'

He leaned back. 'What is the definition of happiness, Aunt?'

'The knowledge that you have done your duty and have done no harm to those around you.'

'That is all?'

'Does there need to be more?'

He tossed the pen to one side. 'I suppose not. But I do wonder what has caused you to visit me with this burning question about Miss Mitchell.'

'Her father was here this morning. What a nightmare of a man.'

Jasper had been aware that his aunt had received a visitor at an unseasonably early hour. He'd been informed of it when he returned from his morning ride, but he had not enquired as to the identity of her caller. He did not interfere with his aunt and he did not expect her to interfere with him. 'I have not met her papa. I am surprised to hear he called on you.'

'You were out.'

He leaned forward in his chair. 'So you agreed to see him in my stead? Don't you think that rather high handed?'

'Jasper, you know I do not poke my nose into your affairs, but he insisted on seeing someone. Caldwell was going to throw him out until I came across them at the front door on my way to breakfast. I had no choice but to smooth his feathers or we would be facing a scandal.'

In his aunt's eyes there was nothing worse than a scandal. The family name must remain unbesmirched, no matter the cost.

'What scandal?'

'She was seen with you at Vauxhall last night.'

He stared down his nose at her. 'She and her chaperon were there at my invitation. She wanted to see the fireworks.'

'You invited her to a masquerade at Vauxhall? Have your wits gone begging? Have I not always warned you to be careful around women of the middle classes? They do not understand the rules of society and nor do their papas. He is insisting that you make her an offer, chaperon or no.'

'You did tell him that the only reputation at risk is his daughter's, I assume.'

Her lips thinned. 'I did. I felt sorry for the poor man when he realised I was right. Personally, I blame the Durant woman.' She closed her eyes briefly. 'It was my fault you fell into her clutches. I have heard things since then that have made me regret the introduction.'

'What sort of things?'

'They say she is very clever at her business. She has manoeuvred more than one man into marriage. No doubt she schemed the whole thing.'

'It is not possible.' It was he who had suggested they attend the masquerade. He pushed a niggling doubt aside. 'Are you now saying you do not like the idea of a match between me and Miss Mitchell?'

Sometimes the female mind was unfathomable. Not sometimes. All the time.

'She is a nice young woman. Quite lovely. With nice manners and a good heart. But to be honest, having met her father, I have my doubts. And I certainly did not wish for you to be forced into marriage by some trick.'

'No one is forcing me into anything.'

'I am pleased to hear it. But do you plan to make her an offer? You really need to make up your mind, Jasper.'

He took a deep breath. 'Leave the matter with me.'

She gave him an encouraging smile. 'I knew I could count on you to do the right thing.'

That was what everyone knew about him. That he always did the right thing. Always did his duty.

'Will I be permitted to waltz tonight?' Charity asked Amelia a little too casually as her maid finished pinning her hair.

Since the Vauxhall debacle, Amelia had resided at the Mitchell town house and would do so for the rest of their stay in London. Clearly, she needed to keep a closer eye on her charges and it would be fair to say that Mr Mitchell was not especially pleased with her. Though it did seem they had escaped any sort of repercussions from that little adventure thanks to Jasper frowning at anyone who even hinted it might not have all been above board and perfectly respectable. Clearly, he was a man who did as he pleased with impunity. A cold chill trickled down her spine at the thought.

Yet…he did not seem to use his power for ill. And he had given up his own pleasure in order to aid Charity. Not something every gentleman would do. Certainly her husband had never given up anything he wanted to do, not even for her sake. According to him, marrying her had been enough of a sacrifice.

Still, the big question in her mind was what Jasper planned with regard to Charity and the future. Because if he did not plan to come up to scratch, then Amelia needed to look elsewhere.

Oh, dear, was that a little bit of hope she felt in her heart?

Tonight being Wednesday, they were off to Almack's Assembly. If Jasper was there, it would give her a chance to thank him properly.

'You may waltz, provided the right gentlemen asks,' Amelia said.

Charity's shoulders slumped. 'You mean the Duke.'

Amelia forced herself to smile gently. 'Not necessarily.'

'What about me?' Patience said. 'I want my first waltz to be with Mr Dobson.'

To Amelia's surprise, Mr Mitchell had given his approval to Mr Dobson's suit. Apparently, he knew Dobson's father. He'd had business dealings with him and thoroughly approved of him, and therefore approved of his son.

'If he is in attendance, I see no reason why you should not waltz with him.'

Patience, who had completed her toilette and now sat on the bed trying not to crease her skirts, beamed. 'He will be there.' The girl glowed.

Whereas Charity looked pale. Almost sickly.

'Do you have a headache, Charity?' Amelia asked. The girl had been looking peaky since they got home from Vauxhall. 'Shall we stay home this evening and attend Almack's next week instead.'

'Oh, you cannot mean that, Mrs Durant,' Patience exclaimed, jumping to her feet. 'What a let down.'

'But if your sister is not feeling quite the thing—'

Charity straightened her shoulders. 'No, indeed. I am well. A little tired, perhaps, but no doubt I shall feel better directly.'

Amelia frowned, then shrugged mentally. Surely the girl would regain her spirits once she was among her friends.

The housekeeper popped her head through the door. 'The carriage is waiting, Mrs Durant,' she said. She beamed at the girls. 'My, don't you ladies look a picture.'

'Thank you,' Amelia replied. She ushered the girls downstairs and out of the front door. She was surprised when Lord Sherbourn stepped into their path. He thrust a bunch of flowers at Charity. 'My humble apologies, Miss Mitchell. I had no intention to cause you distress the other evening.'

Startled, Charity stepped back.

The footman holding the carriage door open for them and waiting to assist them inside lunged forward. 'Step aside, you,' he said thrusting an arm between the young lord and Charity.

Sherbourn turned bright red.

'Oh, Danvers, it is perfectly all right. This gentleman is a friend.'

Sherbourn gave the man a dark look, then must have realised what Charity had said because his brow cleared and he smiled at her shyly. 'You may ever count on me as such, Miss Mitchell.'

'We are going to Almack's,' Charity blurted out. 'Will we see you there?'

He glanced down and winced. 'Not dressed for it, I am afraid. Although—yes, perhaps I shall.'

Amelia refrained from rolling her eyes, though she very much felt like it. The pair of them were so...so... innocent. Had she ever been that way?

Perhaps. In that very first Season, though it was hard to recall that distant time.

Sherbourn dashed off. No doubt to change into knee breeches.

'What is going on?' Papa Mitchell's voice boomed from the open front door. His face was mottled dark red.

'Nothing, Papa,' Charity said.

'You'll have nothing to do with that rascally fellow,' Mr Mitchell boomed on his way down the steps.

'But, Papa,' Charity said, 'he is my friend.'

Papa stuck out a bottom lip. 'If he is such a good friend, he would not have put you in harm's way.'

'Harm's way,' Charity gasped. 'What can you mean.'

Her father glared at her and then at Amelia. 'You know exactly what I mean. She is not to have anything to do with that fellow. Not a thing. Or you will return home in disgrace. Do you understand me, missy?'

Charity was back to looking wan and miserable. 'Yes, Papa. I understand,' she whispered.

'Yes, Mr Mitchell,' Amelia said.

The journey to Almack's was accomplished in silence until just before they arrived. Charity pressed her hands together. 'How can I give him the cut direct, Mrs Durant? He will be so hurt.'

'It would also be seen as extremely rude,' Amelia said. 'Do not worry, I will explain to your father that you must observe the common courtesies or it really will cause a scandal.'

'Thank you,' Charity said, her eyes brimming with tears. 'You are too good and after I played such a trick on you.'

'We all make mistakes, Charity,' she said comfortingly.

'I'll wager you never did anything so foolish,' Patience said.

'Oh, I did.' She'd let a man convince her to go apart with him late at night, knowing full well if she was caught it would bring certain ruin. She'd paid the price for that piece of foolishness. She did not want Charity to suffer the same fate.

The carriage drew to a halt and they climbed

down. They changed into their slippers in the cloak-room and mounted the stairs to the assembly rooms.

There was a short line of people waiting to show their tickets and Charity kept looking over her shoulder. Hoping for a glimpse of Lord Sherbourn, no doubt.

They entered the ballroom and Amelia looked around for Jasper. He was not among the guests, unless he was in the gaming room.

She found a chair with some of the other chaperons and settled down to keep a close eye on her charges.

She was surprised when Sally Jersey joined her a few minutes later. The young woman sat down beside her with a soft sigh. 'I am glad to see you here, Mrs Durant,' she said. 'It would not do to turn tail and run.'

Amelia's heart sank. 'What can you mean, Lady Jersey?'

'The Duke was seen leaving your abode in the early hours of the morning a few nights ago. Speculation is rife.'

The relief that it was not Vauxhall she was speaking of turned to chagrin as she realised the import of the words.

'I—'

'Do not bother denying it, my dear.' She patted Amelia's hand. 'No one will blame you one bit. Stone is a very attractive man and a bachelor to boot. For the time being at least. I have it on good authority he is ready to settle down to the business of marriage. Very good authority.'

Amelia's shoulders stiffened. She forced a pleasant smile. 'I certainly hope you are right. The Season will soon be over and, if Stone does not come up to scratch, I shall be forced to seek an alternative match.'

Sally Jersey nodded. Her gaze rested on Charity, who was as usual the centre of a group of young people who seemed to regard her with awe. Particularly the young gentlemen. 'Do you think Miss Mitchell will make him a good wife?'

Amelia wanted to scream. No, she did not think the girl would make Stone a good wife. Charity would never stand up against his autocratic ways. She would do exactly as he demanded. And no doubt he would be bored to death within the year. But that was not her concern.

What did it matter if she thought neither of them would be truly happy? As long as they rubbed along reasonably well, that was all that was required in a marriage. Truly, she had thought Stone long past the age when his head could be turned by mere beauty, but had not experience taught her that men did not use the head on top of their shoulders when it came to women?

Certainly the world would think her mad if she tried to talk Charity out of the match. Indeed, how could she when she herself had fallen for his charms? People might even accuse her of trying to snare Stone for herself, given the gossip now rife. Besides, what girl would not be happy when offered a coronet of eight strawberry leaves? Papa Mitchell would be in alt.

Yet she had the feeling Charity would far rather

settle for a rather romantic young man named Sherbourn.

But if the Duke had decided to make Charity an offer, what could Amelia do? He must have decided she would suit him. And there was no more to be said.

'Miss Mitchell will make any man a good wife,' she said, ignoring the pain around her heart. After all, it was the truth.

Lady Jersey nodded her agreement and drifted away, leaving Amelia to ponder her future.

Good lord, was she moping about having accomplished the most advantageous match of the Season? Certainly not.

She was thrilled.

Then why did she feel so empty inside?

It did not take Jasper a moment to spot Mrs Durant engaged in deep conversation with Sally Jersey. Whatever they were discussing, the topic seemed to cause Mrs Durant a pang, for she looked distinctly uncomfortable.

Next, his sought out the whereabouts of Miss Mitchell. He simply had to look for the largest clutch of debutantes and their swains to locate her. And of course, she was the reason he was here this evening. He paused, watching her, chatter to her friends. He also noticed the way she continually darted glances towards the door, as if she was expecting someone. Unfortunately, she was going to be disappointed. He'd made sure of it.

The dance in progress, a country dance, was reaching its conclusion.

As he made his way across the dance floor, he had no doubt that everyone present made a note of his arrival and the fact that he had made straight for this Season's most admired beauty. The crowd around Charity parted to let him through.

There were some definite benefits to being a duke.

He bowed over Charity's extended hand. 'Good evening, Miss Mitchell.'

She managed a smile. 'Good evening, Duke.'

'May I have the next waltz?'

She glanced around, visibly swallowed, but nodded. 'Yes. Thank you.'

He breathed a sigh of relief. The first hurdle had been successfully got over. He smiled and nodded at the other members of her group. Looking uncomfortable, they drifted away. 'How are you enjoying this evening?' he asked.

'Very much. Thank you.'

'Good.' Hearing the opening bars of a waltz, he held out his arm.

Like a lamb led to the slaughter, she took it and they moved on to the dance floor. She danced beautifully, light on her feet and her gaze fixed on his face. The fact that her smile was a little stiff would likely be apparent to no one but himself.

'Relax, Miss Mitchell. This is, after all, your first waltz at Almack's. It should be a memorable experience.'

'I am sure it will be, Your Grace.'

'Why so formal, my dear? I thought we were friends.'

She blushed. 'Indeed. You have shown yourself to be a good friend.' She emphasised the word. 'Mrs Durant said I should express my gratitude when next I saw you.'

'It was my pleasure, Miss Mitchell, to extract you from your difficulty the other night and I will not hear another word about it.' He had more important things on his mind.

Her smile eased.

She became more pliant in his arms, more at one with the music. She really was a lovely girl. 'What are your plans for when the Season is over?' he asked.

'I suppose it will depend on what happens,' she said quietly. 'Patience has been invited to spend a few weeks with Mr Dobson's parents in Worthing where they have taken a house for the summer. They invited me also. I am not sure if Papa will agree to us going.'

'Do you like the seaside?'

'I like it well enough.'

'And do you like the country? I have a mind to make up a party at Stone Hall. Three weeks or so of bucolic entertainments for a few select acquaintances.'

A crease formed between her eyebrows. 'Are you inviting me?'

He chuckled. What a delight she was. 'I am feeling my way, Miss Mitchell, seeing if you would prefer a visit to the country over a stay at the seaside.'

'Oh, I see. I have not spent much time in the country.' She smiled shyly. 'I rather think I should like to do both,' she said, smiling. 'Papa was not quite pleased when he realised that the Dobsons did not stay in Bath. I believe he was tempted to refuse. Poor Mr Dobson has been on tenterhooks awaiting his decision. I think Papa might be more inclined to accept their invitation to Patience, if I accepted yours.'

And so she was prepared to martyr herself for the sake of her sister. Her loyalty was admirable and, as always, he found her complete honesty refreshing. He would look forward to her visit. 'You will bring Mrs Durant as your chaperon, of course, and your papa will also receive an invitation, naturally.'

She looked startled. 'You would invite Papa? Are you sure? Oh, I do not think he will come. He hates the country. It is too slow for him. He is a city man.'

'I myself rarely come to town apart from the Season and most years I do not come to London at all unless the business before Parliament is of interest. I am what many call a bit of a hermit.'

He negotiated around the end of the dance floor and gently turned Miss Mitchel beneath his arm, giving her time to think about his words.

Indeed, having absorbed his words, she looked horrified. 'Is that true of all gentlemen?'

He smiled. 'I think you have seen for yourself it is not. But I have several country estates and all demand my attention.'

'I see.'

'I look forward to showing you Stone Hall this summer.'

Her smile faltered, but she caught herself and brightened. 'I am sure I shall enjoy it immensely.'

That remained to be seen.

Chapter Ten

From the corner of her eye, Amelia watched the Duke dance with Charity. He was clearly pleased and if his good friend Lady Jersey was convinced he was about to make her an offer, then Amelia had no doubt that he would.

They made a handsome couple. He so tall and dark and she so dainty and fair. It would be the marriage of the year, if not the decade.

Resolutely, she turned her gaze away and listened to the conversation of the other ladies sitting on the sidelines. They were discussing the latest fashion in widows' caps. She hoped she looked interested for it would not do too be caught staring at Stone. With Charity. People were already gossiping about Stone leaving her house late one night. If they thought she was lovelorn, they would have a field day. And she wasn't. She was worried for them both. But matters were now out of her hands. If the Duke had decided on Charity as his bride, no one, least of all her, could prevent it from happening.

'A penny for your thoughts.'

Her heart leaped at the deep voice so close to her ear. She whipped her head around. 'Stone! You startled me.'

A nearby lady tittered.

Amelia's face heated.

'I beg your pardon, Mrs Durant. I came to request your hand for the next waltz.'

Puzzled, she almost refused, but the intensity in his blue eyes had her changing her mind. 'I shall be delighted.'

He nodded. 'In the meantime, may I bring you some refreshment?'

He was such a kind gentleman. One did not see that about him until one got to know him better. 'Thank you.'

He sauntered off, yet his step had such an aura of purpose, others gave way at his approach. Amelia forced herself not to watch him and once more paid attention to a conversation that had now moved on to the right time to wean a child. Not something about which she had anything to contribute. In her salad days and early in her marriage she had liked the idea of being a mother. Sadly, no issue had resulted from her marital congress.

'My children are such a blessing,' the lady who tittered was saying. 'Never a day passes without one or other of them paying me a visit.'

'How many children do you have?' Amelia asked.

The woman beamed. 'Eight and five grandchildren and another on the way.'

'Your family breeds like rabbits,' one of the other ladies said with a sniff. 'I have two. And that was quite enough for me.'

At that moment, Stone returned with her glass of ratafia. Amelia rose to her feet. After a quick glance to make sure Charity and Patience were back on the dance floor, she smiled at Stone. 'Do you think it might be quieter in the supper room?'

'Without a doubt.'

With both glasses held in one hand, he escorted her out of the ballroom.

'You look troubled, Mrs Durant,' he said once they found a table.

'Oh, dear, and here I thought I was doing such a fine job of hiding my thoughts. The ladies were talking about children and grandchildren. I had not expected to feel envy.'

'It is not too late for you to start a family, surely?'

Men. They simply did not understand the way the clock moved inexorably onwards for a woman. She was well past the age when she would receive an offer of marriage from another nobleman and her family would tolerate nothing less. They only permitted her the licence of living on her own because she never asked them for financial help. With the gossip about her and Stone, she half expected her cousin to come to London and insist she return home to the bosom of what family she had left. It was not how she planned to spend her declining years.

A couple of curious glances from people seated at nearby tables came their way. She sighed. 'I should not be seen in a private *tête-à-tête* with you.'

'Hardly private,' he said, his dark eyes twinkling with something on any other man she might have described as mischief. Clearly, he was thinking of their other private moments. Another blush fired her cheeks.

'Why did you seek me out?'

'I wanted you to know that I intend to invite the Misses Mitchell to my Sussex country house for a summer party.'

Her heart missed a beat. For a second, she felt queasy. It was as if someone had struck her hard in the chest. Sally had been right. He did indeed plan to make Charity an offer.

'You need to consult with Mr Mitchell.'

'Indeed, I will. But I wish to make sure you will be available to serve as chaperon. Aunt Mary will be with us, but honestly she has no idea how to deal with a pair of lively girls like the Mitchell sisters.'

For a moment she could not believe her ears. 'You want me to go, too.'

'I am counting on you.'

So, she was to watch him court Miss Mitchell. But what else could she do? If she did not oversee this part of the match, she could easily lose her fee. Papa Mitchell was a businessman and he would be quick to point out that she had not had a hand in finalising the arrangement between the parties.

There was one thing that needed to be made clear,

however. She lowered her voice. 'You do understand that of necessity, now that you are serious in your intentions, our—dalliance—is at an end.'

'Naturally.'

A hollowness filled her when she ought to be pleased that he was such an honourable gentleman. 'Then if Mr Mitchell agrees to the visit, and he is content to have me act as chaperon, I will agree.'

The Duke raised his glass in a toast. 'To summer house parties. May they prosper for all concerned.'

Drat the man for looking so pleased with himself.

'House parties.' She sipped her ratafia.

He cocked his head. 'I believe they are striking up the next waltz. Shall we?'

Of course Papa Mitchell had been delighted at the idea of his daughters visiting a duke, though he had refused to accept the invitation made to him, citing business affairs keeping him much too busy to be lolling around in fields of cows.

Patience had also been quite indignant at the thought of cutting short her visit with the Dobsons all for the sake of a duke. That was, until she discovered that Mr Dobson had also been invited. After which she had been all smiles and anticipating the treat with a great deal of delight.

Mr Mitchell had not been so pleased when he learned that Amelia was to continue as chaperon to the girls at the Duke's request. A shrewd man of the world, he had eyed her with great suspicion when she informed him. However, after an invitation to dine with the Duke and their after-dinner conversation over brandy and cigars, he became sanguine.

Stone had reported to Amelia the following day that it had been a most edifying conversation. She could only imagine.

Amelia did not go with the girls to Worthing. Lady Dobson was chaperon enough. Instead, she went to visit her family in Cirencester. Three weeks of fetching and carrying for her cousin's wife, who loved the idea of an unpaid servant, was enough to convince Amelia she was doing the right thing in maintaining her independence. It was without regret that she boarded the mail coach bound for London where the Duke had arranged for a post chaise to take her to Stone Hall.

She was the first of his guests to arrive. The view of the house was spectacular when they turned into the drive. She had heard that it was the smallest of the ducal estates. Even so, she had expected it to be grander, somehow. Instead, its seventeenth-century-style roofs, chimneys and dark red brick at one end and the adjoining medieval tower gave it a quaint, cosy appearance. The surrounding park was not more than thirty acres, with ancient trees framing the house to the east and west.

The carriage stopped for her to alight at the front door and then drove away around to the back.

Lady Mary greeted her most kindly and showed her to her room in what she called the new wing.

'Your room lies between that of Miss Mitchell

and Miss Patience,' Lady Mary said, throwing open the door.

It was how she herself would have arranged matters. The room was quite lovely, beautifully decorated in pale green and white, with a four-poster bed against one wall and two armchairs either side of a fireplace with a carved fireplace.

'I hope it meets with your approval?' Lady Mary asked.

'It does indeed. Thank you, Lady Mary. This is most comfortable.'

She strolled over to the window looking out over the park and into the distance. In a valley not far off, the spire of a church rose above the trees and grey roofs signified a nearby village. 'The view is lovely.'

Lady Mary joined her at the window. 'The village of Stonehaven sits on the edge of the park. To be honest, I was surprised when Stone told me he had decided to spend part of the summer here. He has not been here since he was a boy. I was not sure he recalled it at all.'

The puzzlement in the older woman's face made no sense. 'It strikes me as the sort of place that should be lived in.'

'It was, until his parents died. They resided here more than anywhere else. Anyway, it is of no moment. This is where he has chosen to spend the summer.' Another carriage rolled up the drive. 'Ah, more guests arriving. We will gather in the drawing room before dinner. At six. We are keeping country hours while we are here. If you need anything, ring the bell, the housekeeper will be happy to assist.'

She bustled away.

Amelia frowned at the carriage as it slowed and drew up. From this angle, she could not see who alighted. She had neglected to ask who else was to make up the party at Stone Hall. Not that it mattered, she supposed. By the end of the three weeks, the Duke would have made his offer and, once Dobson made his for Patience as he surely would without much delay, Amelia could retire to her cottage in the country as she had planned all along.

Except the idea did not thrill her the way it used to.

His valet helped Jasper into his tight-fitting evening coat. 'Will that be all, Your Grace?'

'It will, thank you, Flynn.'

The valet tidied up the items on the dressing table, while Jasper walked from his bedchamber to the sitting room that adjoined it and poured himself a brandy. He had not visited Stone Hall since he left here shortly after his parents' death. It was the oldest of the ducal estates. The first property the Warren family had owned on their way up the societal ladder to their current exalted social position. Exactly as he had feared, the memory of his parents lived on in every room. Especially the lord's suite. He could recall being allowed to watch his father at his toilette in this suite of rooms on days when his parents had guests.

Why on earth had he decided to invite his guests

here? He had so many other choices. Stoneborough Castle was far more impressive. Yet he had the feeling his prospective bride might well be deterred by its grandeur.

A sharp rap at the door and his Aunt Mary entered. He turned his head and narrowed his gaze on her worried expression.

'What is the matter?'

'I have received a note from Albert.'

His shoulders stiffened. He forced calm into his voice. 'What is it this time?' He'd seemed in fine fettle at Vauxhall.

'A small matter of a debt he will settle at the beginning of the next quarter. Poor lad. The position he obtained did not work out well. A matter of personalities, he said. He is always so unlucky. Unless—'

'I will not pay any more of Albert's debts. He must live within his means the same as the rest of us.'

'But—'

'No, Aunt.' Albert, as Jasper knew to his cost, would not appreciate the generosity one little bit and would likely run up more debt, seeing it as a sign of weakness.

Aunt Mary sighed. 'I will write to him at once and let him know.'

And likely enclose money of her own.

'You know we have not had a visit from him in an age, though the dear boy always writes to me once a week.'

He had not visited because Jasper preferred to keep the 'dear boy' at a distance. He glanced at the clock.

It wanted a quarter of an hour until six. 'I suppose we should go down.'

'Yes, indeed. I informed our guests to gather in the drawing room at six as you requested.'

It would not be polite for guests to arrive and not find their host waiting for them. Jasper held out his arm. 'Shall we?' He escorted her down to the drawing room.

Stone Hall had originally been built as a fortified manor. The lord's chamber was located in the squat tower reached by way of a staircase at one end of the medieval Great Hall, where in times of old his knights would have eaten and slept. Now the Great Hall served as a reception room when guests came to call, and a new wing had been added on the other side some time during the previous century and included a formal dining room and guest bedrooms.

As a child he had loved the romance of this ancient baronial dwelling. As he had so often done as a child when leaving his parents' bedchamber, he stopped halfway down the steps and glanced through the peephole set in the wall, put there so the baron could observe the company without being seen. The lower chamber was empty, but in the old days, when the lord made a grand entrance, he would have been able to see, and more importantly, hear, the interactions between his guests before he went among them. These days, he would no more dream of spying on his visitors than he would dream of running across his lawns naked.

He proceeded down the last few steps and entered the hall with its hammer-beam roof towering some twenty feet above. His steps echoed loudly as he crossed the room to his butler standing beside the console from which refreshments would be served.

'All in readiness, Bedwell?'

'Yes, Your Grace,' the butler said, then gazed straight ahead.

Light poured through the west-facing stained-glass windows. The familial coats of arms cast jewel-like colours on the flagstone floor. Heavy carved chairs were set around the walls. In the centre of the floor one could still see the dark soot stains made by the brazier which would have warmed the room in ancient times. Directly above, if one looked carefully, one could see the hole in the roof through which the smoke would have, eventually, made its way out.

He had played knights and dragons in this room as a child. His father had been the dragon.

Light footsteps in the stone corridor that joined the old wing to the new announced the imminent arrival of some of his guests.

He braced himself. Why the hell was he feeling nervous?

The Mitchell sisters entered with Mrs Durant right behind.

He came forward to meet them. 'Welcome to Stone Hall, ladies. I hope you have found everything to your liking?'

The ladies chorused their greetings and praise for their accommodations. Mrs Durant's smiles and assurances seemed a little forced to his eyes, but he played the good host and soon everyone had a glass of something suitable and he was giving them a brief history of the estate.

'There really is a spy hole?' Charity asked, looking upwards.

'You cannot see it from here,' he said. 'It is very cleverly concealed, but it is hidden among the carvings up there in the corner.'

'Surely, in those days, guests would have expected something of the sort and would have been very careful not to expose themselves,' Mrs Durant said drily.

He laughed. 'My thought exactly. Indeed, it might have been more of a deterrent to conspiracy than a way of uncovering it.'

She looked intrigued. 'I had not considered it from that angle.'

'Can we see it?' Patience asked, just as he had expected she would, of course.

'Most certainly.' He led them through the narrow doorway in the corner of the room and up the stone steps to the small landing with another door into a room, directly below his chamber.

'What is through there?' Patience asked.

Trust her to be curious. 'That is my study. My sanctuary of sorts. I believe at one time it was a solar for the lady of the manor.'

Each lady took a turn looking down into the great hall. While Charity was peering down the angled slit a voice echoed up from below.

'Where is everyone?'

Every word was clear and distinct. She jumped

back. She tottered at the edge of the step and Jasper reach out to catch her elbow before she took a tumble.

'Lord Sherbourn is here?' she gasped as he steadied her.

'Ah, yes. Mr Dobson asked if he might join us, since they are good friends and Sherbourn had no plans for the summer.'

Amelia was looking at him as if he had run mad. Perhaps she would understand better, once he had explained. He hoped.

The evening had passed pleasantly enough, but Amelia had suffered a great deal of anxiety throughout. Now back in her chamber with time to think, she paced back and forth. What on earth had Jasper been thinking in permitting Lord Sherbourn to join their party? He himself had remarked on Charity's interest in the young man and here he was, throwing them together.

Amelia had spent the entire evening trying to make sure Lord Sherbourn did not monopolise Charity, trying to draw his attention to herself until Charity had sent a gaze full of hurt her way.

Good heavens, did the foolish chit think Amelia could possibly be interested in a man at least five years younger than she? What a mess. She needed a word with the Duke of Stone. And the sooner the better.

A rap on the door halted her perambulations. 'Come.'

The sisters' maid, Hooper, bustled in. 'Sorry to be so long, ma'am, we couldn't find Miss Patience's hairbrush. It somehow got to the bottom of the clothes press.'

'That is all right, Hooper, I can ready myself for bed. You must be exhausted after such a busy day.'

The maid had been up since dawn, packing and readying the girls and then unpacking them when they arrived. Still, the young woman looked doubtful. 'I don't mind, Mrs Durant. Truly, I don't.'

Amelia shook her head. 'I am not ready to retire. I have letters to write.'

The maid bobbed a curtsy. 'As you wish, ma'am. I do truly be tired.' She left.

Amelia breathed a sigh of relief and glanced at the clock. Surely Jasper would not be in bed at ten? She really needed to speak to him, before this country house party turned into a disaster.

She waited a few minutes, not wishing to run into Hooper on her way downstairs, then she set out.

There were two places she could look for the foolish man. His study and the library. He had kindly pointed these rooms out to his guests when he had guided them from the Great Hall to the dining room located in the newer wing.

She opted for his study as the first place to look. She knocked and entered.

He was seated behind his desk with a glass of wine in his hand. Oddly, he did not seem surprised to see her on his threshold and pushed to his feet. 'Mrs Durant? Is something amiss?'

'It would seem so, Stone.' She closed the door behind her. When she turned back, he had come around from behind his desk. He was wearing an opulent silk navy blue dressing gown with turquoise dragons. Where it opened at the throat, she could see he had discarded his cravat for a loosely tied neckerchief. He looked relaxed and deliciously attractive.

Her stomach did an odd little flip. Why, oh, why did she find him so alluring? Whenever she had allowed herself to daydream, he'd always popped into her head as a salutary lesson of the sort of man she should avoid. She thought perhaps she might meet and wed a pleasant country squire, who already had his heir and spare, or perhaps a vicar with a congregation where she could do some good. But she'd gone and got herself in a tangle over a duke who saw her only as a passing fancy.

'What brings you to my door at so late an hour?' His deep voice caressed her skin and sent a shiver down her back.

She gritted her teeth against the sensation and the implication in his words. 'Not what you might think.' Her anger at herself made her speak sharply.

He raised an eyebrow at her tone, but seemed unperturbed 'Please, have a seat.' He glanced down at himself. 'I hope you will forgive the informality of my dress. I was not expecting company.'

She waved a dismissive hand, when what she wanted to do was run her hand down his arm and feel the silky fabric against her skin. She seated herself on one of the chairs beside a small table where a game of chess was in progress. White was winning.

'May I offer you a nightcap? Something to help you sleep, perhaps?'

She shot him a glance, but his expression was perfectly innocent. 'Brandy. A little.' It wasn't sleep she needed, but courage.

Now she was here, she wasn't quite sure how to broach the matter on her mind.

He poured them both a glass and sat on the opposite side of the table. 'Do you play?' he asked.

'I do, though I have not for a long while. I used to play with my father.'

He smiled, but there was a hint of sadness in it. 'I also.'

She sipped at the fiery liquid—it had a beautiful aroma and sent warmth sliding down her throat and into her stomach. 'Why on earth did you permit young Sherbourn to join us?'

'Always to the point, eh, Mrs Durant.'

'Well?'

He stared into the amber liquid in his glass. 'There are a couple of maxims I have taken into consideration.'

She frowned.

'The first is, absence makes the heart grow fonder. Were I to separate those two, Miss Mitchell would likely romanticise the young man until he became a knight in shining armour in her mind. I would not like to be married to a woman who fantasised about another man.'

There was some sense to that. And his talking about marriage to Charity struck a tiny blow at her heart. 'And the second?' she said, bracing against more pain.

'Familiarity breeds contempt.'

'You think if she spends a great deal of time in his company, she will tire of him.'

He nodded, then sent her a quizzical look. 'Or she will not.'

'And in that case?'

'My course of action will be clear. What is your opinion? Will her interest in Sherbourn hold true?'

She winced. Was he hurt by this? She hated the idea of him being hurt.

'Only time will tell, I suppose. Personally, while he can be charming, his delight in the dramatics is exhausting. I tire of him after speaking with him for half an hour.'

He chuckled, his eyes dancing with a sort of boy-ish mischief. 'That does not surprise me.'

'I must say, however, if you had wanted to woo Charity with what you have to offer in comparison to Lord Sherbourne, you might have invited her to one of your larger estates.'

'Something more impressive, you mean.'

'Certainly something more ducal. Where footmen stand in every hallway and the dining room table seats fifty.'

He frowned. 'Aunt Mary said much the same thing. But I would prefer my future wife to know the man behind the title. Stone Hall is the place I think of as home.'

She blinked. 'You intend to live here after your marriage?'

'It is where the children of my family always grow up.'

Children. The word caused her stomach to twist painfully. Already he was talking of children. With Charity. But that was the whole idea, was it not? For a duke to marry and have children?

'So, what is your plan? To show Lord Sherbourn up for the young idiot that he is?'

'Something of the sort.' He reached out a hand. 'Will you help me?'

'I do not like the idea of tricking the young man into doing something stupid or dangerous.'

'Certainly not. Given enough rope, a man can hang himself. He already came close with the debacle at Vauxhall. No doubt there will be many opportunities for another such incident in the coming weeks. All I need from you is to curtail your very natural desire to help him avoid disaster when you see it coming and let me slay the dragon. Dragons come in many shapes and sizes.'

And the pitfalls for a young woman like Charity, one with no claim to nobility, were many. 'I see.'

'So, will you stand back and let things take their course?'

'As long as there is no chance of her falling into disgrace, I shall not go out of my way to aid Lord Sherbourn avoid a comeuppance.'

Strangely, a look of disappointment crossed his face. No. She was mistaken. He looked perfectly sanguine. Perhaps even pleased. Well, he would, if he was determined to make Charity a duchess. Which it seemed he did.

And what woman could resist the Duke of Stone once his mind was made up? Certainly not Charity. She was far too biddable. If her papa insisted, then she would do as she was told and make the best of it.

Just as Amelia had done when she married Durant.

Jasper, on the other hand, would make an exemplary husband. He would care for Charity to the best of his ability. It would be the perfect match.

Would it not?

'Another brandy?' he asked.

She looked down at her glass and realised it was empty.

She should not. But she felt so empty, so sad, at this moment, why not? Perhaps it was sleep she needed and everything would look much better in the morning.

Chapter Eleven

So, Amelia was as determined to marry him off to the elder Miss Mitchell as was Aunt Mary. Unfortunately, the maxims he had quoted applied equally to him. The more time he spent in the young lady's company, the less enamoured he became.

A duke married for duty. He married, sired heirs and administered the duchy not for himself, but for the dynasty laid down by his forefathers. Happiness was not a word in his lexicon.

While the duchy was not in financial difficulties, the addition of the sort of wealth that Miss Mitchell would bring to the coffers would not go amiss. Things happened, as he'd discovered over the years. Crops failed. Investments turned bad. Dukes died before they provided their spare. Sometimes before they provided an heir. All of these things had been drummed into him since he was a lad. He knew where his duty lay.

He rose and collected the decanter from the console.

'What about us?' he asked lazily, coming back to top up her glass.

'Us?' Her hand shook. A drop of liquid splashed on the back of her hand.

He took the glass, captured her hand and brought it to his lips, licking away the little drop of moisture. 'Yes, us.'

She snatched her hand back and glared at him, yet deep in those dark mysterious eyes he sensed longing.

'There is no "us".' Scorn coloured her tone. 'Once you are married—'

'Once I am married is a horse of a different colour,' he murmured, tracing his thumb along the delicate angle of her jaw. Tiny littles bumps rose on her skin along her collarbone. 'But at the moment we are both single adult people who take pleasure in each other. Very great pleasure, from my perspective.'

She sighed, then brushed his hand away. 'You are as good as betrothed and—'

'As good as? I hardly think so, my dear. Though I would agree a betrothal is as binding as marriage.' He stroked her cheek with his thumb and handed her the glass of brandy.

She took a sip. Or rather a gulp.

'You wish to continue our affair.'

'It would please me a great deal if you would.'

'And in the meantime, you wish me to promote your suit with Charity.' She smiled wryly.

'Put that way, it sounds rather uncomfortable. So, no. I do not wish you to speak on my behalf. Or against Sherbourn for that matter. What I want is for us to enjoy each other for a few short weeks of the summer until the reality of our situations intrude.'

'Until you are betrothed.'

'Precisely.'

'If you ever are. I mean, with Lord Sherbourn competing for her attention while you as host must attend to all your guests equally, I think you will have your work cut out for you.'

'It will be a case of "may the best man win".'

She narrowed her eyes on him as if she did not believe him.

She did not like to feel as if her hand was forced. The way her shoulders stiffened he sensed a refusal. 'I beg your pardon, Mrs Durant. I do not wish to make things difficult for you. Please feel free to reject my offer. I shall not hold it against you, my dear, though I shall be disappointed.'

She turned her head from him, staring at a landscape on the wall nearby. It seemed that he had been mistaken in thinking she had enjoyed his attentions as much as he had enjoyed hers. Either that or her moral compass was far truer than his. 'I beg—'

'Yes,' she said.

He stilled.

'Yes, I would like us to continue our intimacies,' she added, clearing up any doubts he might have had as to her meaning in her usually decided manner.

He took her hand and brought her to her feet. 'You cannot know how…' He hesitated. Was this the sort of occasion when one could use the word happy? Was

* * *

Amelia let his kiss carry her into the hot, dark, warm depths of passion. All her doubts were subsumed by the delight of his lips on hers, his large hands wandering her person and the feel of his body flush against hers. And the fact that he would call her lovely—well, it made her melt inside.

She had always been attracted to him, even when he had looked right through her, but now she found him irresistible. The knowledge that their time together must be brief gave her an unexpected sense of urgency. A need to enjoy the moments to the full before he would be gone from her life for ever.

She kissed him with fervour, running her hands over his strong wide shoulders, through his hair, down his spine, learning the shape of his body beneath the slick silk of his dressing gown. Kissing him was a delight. His mouth was soft, wooing, his tongue delicate in its explorations, his hold on her firm, yet gentle. Her insides turned liquid, her limbs felt heavy. Her legs trembled until she feared they might give way.

As if sensing her weakness, he picked her up and carried her to the armchair beside the hearth. He sat down, settled her on his lap and the kiss began anew. Why had she not known a simple kiss could be so extraordinary? That it could rob one of breath and strength and reason. No wonder papas never left their daughters alone with young men. She could not help but feel a pang of envy for Charity, who would soon be the recipient of his kisses.

How foolish of her to think of that at this moment. If she wanted this, with him, she had to live in the here and now and enjoy the banquet she was offered. Because it would soon be off the table. She was an honourable woman. No matter how she felt, she would never vie for the affections of a man committed to another.

She slid her hand under his lapel, stroking the fine linen of his shirt, and, finding the button undone, trailed her fingers over warm flesh made rough by crisp curls of hair. He made a guttural sound of pleasure in response to her touch. Between her thighs, deep inside, her body tingled. She tightened and gasped at the hint of the visceral pleasure that would soon be hers.

Ever since their last encounter, she only had to think about his hands on her body and waves of pleasure would work outwards from her core. The intensity was all the greater when he was here in person. Heat washed through her. She turned towards him, pressing her breasts against his chest, sliding her hand upwards and around his neck, between him and the chair back, pulling him into her, wanting closer contact.

He groaned and shifted beneath her and she felt the hard ridge of his arousal against her bottom. He broke their kiss. 'This is no good.'

Horrified, she stared at him. She had thought it perfect.

He swept and impatient hand through his hair. 'I refuse to make love to you jammed in this dashed chair.'

Oh. That. 'The floor?' The carpet looked plush enough, she supposed.

'Absolutely not, when I have a perfectly good bed nearby. It seems we must do some creeping after all.'

She chuckled at the disgruntlement in his voice. 'Wheresoever you lead, will I follow.'

He smiled down at her, his expression softening. 'I truly like the sound of that.' He helped her off his lap and, taking her hand, led her to the door. 'Fortunately for us, none of the servants occupy the old part of the house so we are unlikely to run into anyone. Most of them don't like to come here after dark.'

'Why on earth not?'

'Ghosts have been sighted.' There was a sepulchral ring to his voice along with an edge of amusement.

'Really? Surely you do not believe in such things?'

'Me? Of course not. Er… I may have had a hand in the rumours, though.'

Her eyes rounded. 'What did you do?'

It had been years ago when he was little more than twelve, not long before his parents died. 'I clanked a few chains and made some scary noises. The house-keeper in those days was very superstitious. She embellished what she had heard into something she had seen. She refused to believe it was all done by me, even when Father made me confess the whole.'

'And the rumours continue?'

'They do. Last time I heard there is a headless lady and a sword-wielding Viking roaming the halls at night. The only person unaffected by the gory tales is my valet. But since I already dismissed him for the night, he will not bother us.'

He unlocked the door and took her hand.

They took the stone steps, up past the peephole, to the landing above and into a large chamber with a window that matched the one in the Great Hall. She had noticed it when she arrived, but had not thought about in which room it might be located. Cushions in multi-coloured hues lined the bench set within the window embrasure and a candelabra with ten branches burned on the windowsill.

The square linenfold-panelled room had clearly been built around the same time as the grand hall. The windows up here were decorated with a pastoral scene, rather than with coats of arms, and the plaster ceiling had been decorated with Tudor roses and quatrefoils. A large four-poster bed on a raised dais occupied the wall opposite the windows. It was like stepping back in time.

'I can see why your servants might think it haunted,' she remarked. 'And you actually sleep here?'

'I do. Not that I have spent much time here since I was a lad. Too many memories of my parents.'

'You do not like to be reminded of your parents?'

He pulled her deeper into the room and briefly kissed her lips, the tip of her nose and then nuzzled his way down her neck.

Shivers ran across her shoulders and down her back.

The scent of his cologne, something earthy with

an undertone of spice, enveloped her. She inhaled deeply as if by doing so she could keep the memory of it locked away… But he had not answered her question. Indeed, it seemed he was trying his best to make her forget it. She knew that his parents had died when he was young. Was he still grieving for them so painfully after all this time? How sad.

'I think it a beautiful room. Full of history. And certainly romantic enough for a lover of Ann Radcliffe. Are there any secret passages or tunnels, do you know?'

'Nary a one. I spent a long time looking for one as a boy, but the only secret is the peephole, sad to say.' He gave her a quizzical look. 'I hope you are not too disappointed.'

She grinned at his teasing. 'Not at all. Indeed, this house is a charming mix of old and new.'

He smiled. 'I am glad you think so.' His expression warmed as he gazed at her. An answering heat rose up from her belly.

'May I take down your hair?' he asked. 'I would love to see it loose about your shoulders.'

Her hair was her crowning glory, even if she said so herself. It complemented her darker skin tone, though her schoolmates had turned their noses up at her dusky complexion.

While Jasper was surprised at her easy acceptance of his suggestion that she join him in his bedroom, he could not be more pleased. He had expected to have to work a great deal harder to woo her into his bed. But then she was a woman who knew what she wanted. And what she didn't want.

One by one he removed the pins from her plain coiffure, waiting in heady anticipation for the moment when it would fall free to her shoulders. No fussy little ringlets spoiled the view of her brow or hid the delicate blue veins at her temples. Unlike her charges, the Mitchell sisters, there was nothing pretty about her at all. A simple plait around a glossy bun at the back of her head provided an uninterrupted view of glorious planes and angles of a face that had strength as well as a unique beauty.

Again, he regretted that he did not recall her from her first Season.

With infinite slowness, the twist of hair unravelled and, loose of its confines, slid down her back in a wing of straight midnight black. Two plaits framed her face. He unravelled them, running the silky softness through his fingers until they fell in soft waves to cover her breasts. 'You have the most beautiful hair,' he murmured.

'Most gentlemen prefer a true English beauty, blonde hair and pale skin.' She sounded amused, but there was a defensive note in her voice.

'Most gentlemen are idiots.'

'I will not disagree.'

He smiled at her prosaic response and tipped her chin with his forefinger. 'Now it is your turn.'

A puzzled frown formed a crease between her midnight eyebrows. 'For what?'

'To make a request of me.'

She looked intrigued, touched a hand to her hair and nodded. A naughty smile curved her lips and his blood ran hot.

'I would see you stretched out, shirtless and face down, on that bed.'

That he had not expected. 'Your wish is my command.'

She rose on her toes and touched her lips to his. 'You may regret such an offer, Jasper.'

Hmm. He could scarcely imagine anything she could do that would cause him regret. He went for the tie at his waist.

She brushed his hands away. 'Let me.'

Oh, yes. 'With pleasure.'

Too slowly she unknotted the belt and slid the dressing gown off his shoulders and down his arms to pool on the floor at his feet.

He raised an eyebrow as she perused him slowly. He wore only his shirt tucked into his pantaloons, where his erection would be very evident to her gaze. Rarely did his lust betray him in this manner, but tonight was different. He wanted her to know how much he desired her.

That naughty smile broadened and her fingers got busy with the knot in his neckerchief. It followed the dressing gown to the floor and she set to work on the buttons of his shirt. His belly clenched at the feel of her small fingers against his skin as she eased the buttons through the holes and spread the shirt apart to reveal his chest.

'Most impressive,' she said, gazing at him.

He felt like preening, like a lad being praised for some feat of strength. He went to pull his shirt free of his waistband, but once more she brushed his hands aside. 'I feel like I am opening a special present. Let me do it.'

He quelled a laugh at the serious expression on her face. Serious and sensual. He wanted to take the small hand pulling the linen free of his pantaloons, press it against his erection and move in her palm. It took strength of will to resist that temptation. He gritted his teeth and let her pull the fabric free. The feel of the fabric brushing against his skin sent a shiver down his spine.

Finally, the sensual torture ended and she lifted the hem of his shirt. 'Bend for me,' she murmured. When he did so, she pulled the shirt off over his head.

She walked around him, with a considering expression. 'My memory did not fail me. You are magnificent.'

'Good heavens, woman. You sound as if you are reviewing a stallion you plan to purchase,' he grumbled, feeling a little embarrassed by her enthusiastic endorsement.

Her dark eyes turned hazy and her lips took on a sensual cast, as if he had struck some sort of erotic fantasy. She pointed to the bed.

He grinned and sauntered over to the bed, even though he felt like running. This had been his parents' room once upon a time. The thought gave him a pang. He missed them. All these years, thinking about them had made him angry. Furious. But tonight, he felt saddened that their lives had been cut short.

Some wildness inside him made him take a flying leap on to the bed instead of making a stately ascent up the steps as he had been taught. The same wildness that had prompted him these past many days to take risks he would have described as foolish not so very long ago.

She gasped and then laughed. 'Oh, my word. Now you are showing off.'

He glanced over his shoulder and grinned at her. 'Face down? Are you sure? I would much rather look at your lovely face.'

She pouted. 'You did say it was my turn.'

He liked the way she stood up to him. Loved it. No one ever stood up to him. He lay down as instructed. 'Have at it, madam.'

'Oh, I will.' The husky note in her voice caused his ballocks to tighten. He swallowed a groan. Still, his shoulders tensed in anticipation as she crossed the room, her feet a whisper on the carpet.

The steps beside the bed creaked as she climbed up to sit beside him. He shifted over to give her space. Something light and delicate trailed its way down his spine. A fingernail. The muscles across his back jumped. 'Nice,' he murmured.

'You like that?'

'Indeed.'

She continued to run her nail in circles here and there across his shoulders and lower back. 'You are very sensitive to touch,' she observed.

'Mmm. It tickles. If you stroke with the flat of the hand, I would like it even more.'

To his delight, she did as requested.

Then she drew a symbol with her fingertip.

'Why are you making shapes?' he asked.

'Can you tell what they are?'

'A circle and a square.'

'Oh, right. What about this.'

He frowned at the rapid succession of line squiggles ending with what he could only describe as a poke.

'Well?' she said, sounding mischievous.

'Are those letters? And a full stop? You wrote a sentence on my back?'

She giggled. 'Yes. Could you tell what I said?'

'Do them slower.'

She scrubbed his back as if to erase what she had already printed there. This time her finger moved slowly. The pleasure of her touches across his back made it difficult to focus on the shape of her drawings. Some letters were easy and helped him guess at the others.

'You. Are. A. Na… Er…something ending in "y". Boy.'

She laughed 'One more try.' She redrew the word starting with 'n'.

'Naughty. You are a naughty boy.' He laughed, rolled over and pulled her on top of him. 'You haven't seen me anything like naughty as yet.'

She gazed down into his face. 'But no doubt I will.'

He flipped her on to her back and gazed down

at her. 'No doubt at all, my dear Amelia. Starting right now.'

He kissed her and revelled in the way she returned the kiss. The dart of her little tongue in his mouth, the warm wandering hands over his bare back. The feel of her black locks running over his skin as he cupped her face in his hands.

She made him feel alive and excited beyond endurance.

He pushed up on his elbows and gazed down at her. 'I am so glad you came to find me tonight.'

Her face turned serious. 'So am I,' she whispered. 'Wrong though it may be.'

His heart stumbled. 'You believe we are wrong to take pleasure in each other when neither has any commitments or ties?'

Doubt filled her gaze. 'I do not know.'

'If this makes you uncomfortable, you should leave. I do not want you to do anything you do not wish to do.'

She stroked his arm, watching her hand make its way down from his shoulder to his elbow where it pressed into the counterpane. 'It is not that I do not wish to...'

'Then what troubles you?'

'I suppose it is the strength of my feelings when I hold you in my arms. The knowledge that it cannot last.'

Her words sent his heart soaring.

'Is it possible to put such worries aside and simply live for the moment, my sweet darling?'

Her gaze softened, her expression easing. 'Just this once, then.'

It was not quite what he meant, but he nodded. 'If that is your wish.'

For a second, he thought he saw tears pool in her gaze, but she was smiling. He must be mistaken. She reached up and pulled his head down for a kiss.

Chapter Twelve

Amelia gave herself over to his kisses. This would be the last time she would be with him. From tomorrow forward, she would assist him in his wooing of Charity. She could not do her job, not while she was entertaining herself in the Duke's bed. It simply went against her conscience.

Knowing that tonight would be their last night together eased her guilt, yet the feeling of loss was almost unbearable.

When his hand lightly caressed her breast and his heavy thigh pressed down between hers, she arched into him. When that hand roamed downwards and began tugging her skirts upward, she lifted up her hips.

He broke the kiss. 'May I help you out of your gown?' he asked softly.

He helped her to sit up and, with the skill of a lady's maid, soon had her divested of her gown and stays, leaving her only in her shift. He ran his finger around the lace at the neck, brushing the rise of her breasts above her nipples, then leaned forward and licked at the peak. The little nub furled where it pressed against the fabric.

Liquid heat trickled through her core. She gasped at the tightening sensation within her. He did the same to the other breast. It felt so good. She ran her palm across his nipple and delighted in the way it, too, pebbled beneath her fingers.

Once more, he lowered his head to stroke her breast with his tongue, and then, to her shock, he sucked. A pleasurable sensation shot from the tip of her breast all the way down to the place between her thighs. She moaned at the shock of it.

He paid the same attention to her other breast, attending to each one in turn until she thought she would never survive the unbearable tightening inside her. While he teased and tormented her with his mouth, he rocked his hips, pressing his erection against her thigh She reached between them and took the hard ridge of flesh in her hand, squeezing in time to his rocking. He moaned. 'Yes, sweetheart. Oh, yes.'

She wanted more of him. Somehow, despite the pleasure darting through her body from his delicate manipulation of her breasts, she managed to undo the buttons of his falls and set his erection free. The heat of his flesh in her hand, the soft silky texture of the skin with the steely hardness beneath, stole her breath.

She pushed at his shoulder. 'I want to see,' she said.

He raised his head, his eyes barely focused, but

he smiled and rolled on to his back. 'Look your fill, sweetling, but don't delay too long. I find I am anxious to come inside you and bring us both to completion.'

She was anxious, too, but she wanted to see him. To remember him like this when she was alone in her bed with her memories.

He was a magnificent man. The head of his swollen erection reached all the way to his belly button. He pushed at the base with two fingers and made it stand away from his body, stiff and proud, the heavy ropey veins dark with blood a lacy pattern beneath the skin. She knelt astride him and slowly lowered herself down on to the hot flesh.

He filled her and stretched her, and felt so good inside her. Then he rubbed his thumb against her at the place where their bodies joined. If she had thought the feel of his suckling was unbearable pleasure, this little movement of his thumb was sublime. Her insides tightened around his shaft and he hissed out a breath, gently moving inside her, encouraging her to move in counterpoint to his thrusts by lifting her and then pressing her down.

She picked up the rhythm. 'Like posting on a horse.'

He chuckled breathlessly. 'Oh, yes. Ride me, darling.'

Oh, good Lord, she had said that out loud.

Now she had the way of it, his hands lifted to her breasts and caressed them, and toyed with her nipples. Pleasure became an excruciating tightness. An impossible barrier. His clever fingers returned to the tiny spot in front of where their bodies joined. This time, it really was more than she could bear. About to protest, the barrier broke and she shattered, even as she felt him stiffen beneath her, then pull free of her body with a shuddering cry.

She collapsed on his chest and, as he stroked her and murmured sweet words in her ear, she fell asleep.

It was even better than the first time. Bliss-filled contentment left Jasper fighting to remain awake.

With what remained of his will, he grabbed the edge of the counterpane and folded it over her and himself. It would serve as a cover. He did not want her getting cold. Sleep dragged him under.

When next he awoke, she was curled in his arms, her soft bottom pressed against his groin, one of his hands cupping her breast and the other draped over the lovely dip of her waist. He nuzzled her neck. 'It is time we returned you to your room,' he murmured in her ear.

She stirred and stretched out her legs. 'Yes. I must go.'

She relaxed.

'Sweetheart,' he said. He squeezed her breast. 'I love having you here, but soon the servants will be up and about.'

She shot upright, looking around her. A hand went to her mouth. 'Oh, my word. For a moment, I thought I was dreaming.'

It had felt like a dream to him, too.

'A nice dream, I hope?'

A smile curved her plush red lips. 'Lovely. No, better than lovely. Marvellous.'

His heart swelled. He dropped littles kisses on her cheek, her chin, her lips. 'Marvellous indeed.'

He slid off the bed and helped her down. With the light of the last remaining candle bathing her naked skin, she looked ethereal.

He took her hand and kissed it. 'You are so beautiful. I hate to let you go.'

She flushed. 'Thank you. I shall never forget our time together.'

'Nor I.' He leaned in to kiss her.

She placed her hands flat on his chest. 'But, Jasper, this must never happen again.'

Her words rung with finality. Pain tightened his chest. He reached for lightness. 'Never say never.'

She dodged his lips and shook her head. 'No, I mean it. We cannot continue this way now that you are truly courting Charity.'

She was an honourable woman. How could he fault her? 'Very well. If that is your wish.'

'Not my wish, but my decision. You must see that I am right.'

'I understand.'

Slowly, deliberately, he helped her dress. Soon, she looked exactly as she had when she first arrived in his study. Coolly detached. Armoured against the world. Except for the way her black hair rioted about her shoulders, tempting his fingers to rake through the heavy tresses.

As if sensing his thoughts, she turned to the mirror and braided first one side then the other into thick plaits. Fascinated, he watched her skilful fingers tug and wind each strand in turn.

Coming to his senses, he picked up the discarded pins and handed them over one at a time.

She offered him a wry little smile. 'Thank you.'

Did she regret her earlier words about this being the last time?

'Ready?' he asked.

She jerked her head in assent. Decisive with a tinge of bravery.

He walked her down to his study. The servants never came to his wing of the house until he rang for his valet. However, there was no guarantee that some maid or other would not be about her work in the other wing.

He picked up a book from his desk. 'Having awoken in the night, you went looking for a book, I expect.'

She took it. 'Yes, it is the sort of thing one does when one cannot sleep.'

They chuckled. He hugged her and opened the door. 'I will accompany you as far as the Great Hall. You can find your way from there, I hope?'

'Indeed, I can.'

He gazed down into her eyes. 'Would you care to ride out with me in the morning? Say at nine?'

'Miss Mitchell will not be up by then.'

'I understand that.'

A black eyebrow winged upwards. 'Then…'

'We will take a groom, of course. And observe all the proprieties. I understood you to say you are an early riser and that you like to hack out.'

For a long moment she hesitated. 'Yes. I would like that. Actually, Miss Mitchell does not ride, though Patience does, but it would be a chance to discuss the plans for our entertainment over the next few weeks.'

Now she was all business. Her way of pounding in the point that this idyll of theirs had ended.

'My thoughts, exactly. I would have your approval for what I have in mind. And perhaps your assistance. Aunt Mary is getting a bit long in the tooth to rush about organising things, poor dear.'

'I shall be happy to help.'

Would she be equally happy to see him married off?

At the stone arch on the far side of the Great Hall, he bowed. 'I look forward to seeing you later.'

She bobbed a little curtsy. 'Thank you.'

He sighed and strode back to his bedchamber. What a difficult woman she could be. He was never quite sure what to expect.

Amelia hesitated inside the door leading to the stable yard the next morning. Her heart thundered in her chest and grasshoppers seemed to leap about in her stomach. She swallowed the dryness in her mouth. What would he say? How would he look at her after their night of debauchery? She wished she had said no to this outing.

She forced herself to step outside. The sun was already high, the sky blue with the odd white fluffy cloud. A gentle breeze teased at her riding habit. Across the courtyard, a groom and a stable boy held the bridles of two horses, a large bay and a black, while the Duke inspected the saddle of a finely boned brown mare wearing a side saddle.

As if sensing her presence, he straightened and turned, squinting against the sun. A smile broke out on his face at the sight of her, not the smile of a lover, as she had feared, but the smile of a friend. The tension in her shoulders eased.

She returned his smile and strolled to his side. 'She's lovely. What is her name?'

'Pepper. She's good-natured, but she can be a little hot to handle if not worked regularly.' He ran a hand down the mare's neck and she tossed her head and rolled her eyes.

Amelia stroked Pepper's nose. 'Easy, lady.'

Jasper lowered his voice. 'I wondered if you might change your mind.'

Her heart gave an odd little thump at the pleasure in his voice. 'That would be cowardly.'

'You are certainly not that.' He turned. 'Jessup, give us a hand here, would you?'

The groom handed the bay over to the boy, who looked too small to hold such large beasts, but who seemed unfazed by the task. He steadied the mare while the Duke bent and boosted Amelia into the saddle.

The mare didn't move a muscle while Amelia settled her foot into the stirrup and arranged her skirts. She leaned forwards and patted Pepper's neck. 'Good girl.'

Pepper flicked her ears and sidled.

Jasper laughed. 'She'll test you.'

'That is all right. I like a horse with a bit of spirit.' It had been ages since Amelia had hacked out. Before her marriage. Her husband had provided a carriage, but not a riding horse. And now she was widowed, she neither owned a horse nor a carriage. The cost was prohibitive. She had far more important things on which to spend her money.

Besides, who needed a carriage, when all of her clients were more than happy, either to let her stay with them during the time of their contract, or were willing to provide her with transport?

Jasper swung up on to his horse and took up the reins. Goodness, but the man was a fine sight on a horse. The bay playfully tossed his head and danced sideways.

Jasper controlled him without effort.

'Full of vim and vigour this morning,' he remarked to Jessup.

The man touched his hat. 'Didn't get him out for a run yesterday, Your Grace. We put all our attention to the ladies' mounts and the carriage horses, as you requested.'

'Good.' He patted his horse's neck. 'Riptide will settle down once I let him have his head.'

He swivelled in his saddle. 'I hope you don't mind if we start off at a good pace, Mrs Durant? I am sure Pepper there won't be averse to a bit of a canter.'

The horse pricked her ears and nodded her head as if understanding exactly what was being said. The bay pawed at the cobblestones as if anxious to be off.

'I don't see why not, as long as you don't lead me over any fences.' She glanced up to the second floor. Her maid had assured her that both girls were still abed when she had left to come down to the stables. While Charity would be more than happy not to have been invited, Patience was another story. 'I hope you will invite the girls to go riding with you another day.'

He swung his horse around so it lined up beside hers. 'If you think it is the sort of entertainment they would like. I usually ride out at eight. I try to visit one of my neighbours or tenants every day and some of them are quite far distant, but I enjoy having company. I haven't been to this estate in years, it is time I started making amends. I plan to call in on one of them this morning, if you do not mind?'

'Do you usually ride out alone?'

'It depends on where I am, the day and the weather. Sometimes my bailiff joins me. It is a way to get business done as well as engage in healthy exercise.'

The groom mounted up.

Jasper gave his horse the off and they trotted out of the stable yard and along a path leading around the wide expanse of lawn at the back of the house.

Once clear of the gardens, Jasper looked over at Amelia. 'Today I would need to call in on the miller. He has requested a word with me to discuss some matter or other.' His horse wrestled the bit. 'I am going to canter for a bit. If you prefer not, I will wait for you at the end of the drive.' He let the big bay have its head and shot off.

Mindful that she had not been up on a horse for some time, Amelia eased Pepper into a canter and the mare picked up her speed without attempting to race the other horse. The groom's black thundered past her at a gallop.

When she reached the end of the drive the two men were walking the horses out.

'That took a bit of the dash out of the old boy's step,' Jasper said as she reined in beside him.

'He is fast.'

'Yes. I thought about racing him at one time, but he's not competitive enough. Besides, I like to ride him myself.'

Racing. Ugh. 'It is a dangerous sport.'

'Indeed. And I have too many responsibilities to go risking my neck for a bit of fun.'

She wished her husband had had that much sense.

They turned out of the gate at the end of the drive and trotted along the lane for a short distance until the groom went ahead of them and opened a gate.

'We'll take a short cut,' Jasper said. 'I will take you and our other guests on an outing to the village later in the week, but if we go through there today, we are likely to run into too many people and never make it to our destination.'

They walked the horses across the first field, took the next at a canter and passed into a small wood. He gestured with his whip at a fork in the trail. 'If we take this fork we can come at the mill from the other side of the village.'

'Is the village on your land?'

'It is. It seems to me everyone who lives there has a complaint that their landlord must hear and sort out immediately. I get letters from them constantly.'

He sounded so rueful, she laughed. 'My father used to say much the same thing. Owning land is a big responsibility.'

'And costly.'

Was that why he was interested in an heiress for a bride? Could it be that the Duke's financial situation was not what it appeared? Some of the oldest and most noble families of England had married outside their ranks to refill their coffers after years of squandering their fortunes at the gaming tables. She had heard nothing of the sort about Stone. Perhaps she ought to dig a little deeper.

The warmth of the day dissipated. She repressed a shiver and was glad when they emerged into the sunshine once more. A stream cut across the next field and they forded it at a shallow spot. As they climbed the bank on the opposite side, the mill came into view. From the small house beside it, a rotund man with bushy white eyebrows and a florid complexion emerged to meet them.

Jasper dismounted and helped Amelia down. The groom led the horses off to drink from the trough not far from the church gate.

'Mrs Durant, allow me to present our Mr White.'

The man's bow was perfunctory. 'Ma'am.'

'What is the problem, White, that you must send an urgent message to London? If it is about repairs, you should be applying to my man of business, not to me.'

White glanced at Amelia and a bitter smile twisted his lips. 'I think not, Your Grace.' His tone was barely civil.

Jasper frowned. His jaw hardened.

It was an expression Amelia recognised. Haughty and cold. 'Go on.'

White again looked at Amelia. His faced reddened, making the red mottling on his cheeks turn purple. The man looked like he might have an apoplexy at any moment. 'It is personal, Your Grace.'

Jasper frowned, then nodded. He smiled at Amelia. 'If you will excuse us?'

'Of course.' She wandered down to the edge of the millpond out of earshot. There were bulrushes along the edge and marsh marigolds in the grass. A lark warbled its melody high above and Amelia stared upwards, scanning the sky, trying to spot the tiny bird who made such extraordinarily loud music, to no avail.

The voices behind her grew in volume, then cut off abruptly.

She glanced over her shoulder. The miller glowered at the Duke from beneath lowered eyebrows.

'Aaar, she might be called lucky, but fair is fair. I deserves better than…' He lowered his voice, but Amelia, who was desperately trying not to listen, was sure she heard the word 'marriage'.

A few moments later, Jasper broke away, calling out to the groom to bring the horses as he walked away. Amelia strode to meet him.

The groan and creak of the great waterwheel and the splash of water did nothing to drown out the miller's parting shot. 'I'll see right done, Your Grace, so I will.'

He went inside and slammed the door shut.

Amelia gave Jasper an enquiring glance. He stared straight ahead, his lips in a thin straight line, his eyes icy. He clearly did not intend to offer an explanation. Once more the groom followed at a distance, far enough back to offer them privacy and yet keep them in sight.

Who was the 'she' the miller had mentioned and what wrong had she suffered? Amelia tried not to jump to conclusions, but she did not like the Duke's frosty reaction to the miller's problem. Even such a lowly man deserved the respect of a fair hearing. It put her in mind of the way Jasper had treated her, after the first time they met. Perhaps he had not changed as much as she thought.

Had his contempt for the lower orders led him to take advantage of the miller's daughter?

Her stomach fell away. And not only because he had so easily charmed his way into her bed. As a widow, she had nothing to lose by her association with the Duke. A miller's daughter, on the other hand, was entirely vulnerable.

If this suspicion of hers proved was true, how could she in all conscience promote a match between him and Charity?

Chapter Thirteen

Jasper could scarcely contain his fury. Albert was up to his tricks—again. And for some reason, the miller had decided to lay the problem at Jasper's door, as if he were the guilty party. A breach-of-promise suit? He shook his head. Whatever Albert had promised the girl, Jasper would not be drawn into the debacle, no matter how Aunt Mary pleaded. Surely it was time the man took responsibility for his own actions. He took a deep breath and reined in his anger. Amelia was looking at him with a sceptical glint in her eye. How much of his conversation had she overheard?

'I apologise,' he said, forcing calm into his voice as they rode down the lane heading for home. 'When I received his request to call in, I assumed it would be a matter of a broken strut or the need for a new wheel. His message did not indicate the personal nature of the matter.'

She gave him a wry smile. 'Hopefully you were able to allay his concerns?' She did not sound particularly hopeful. Indeed, she sounded rather grim. She glanced up at the sky. 'Do you think this weather will hold for a few days? I hear there are some interesting ruins hereabout and I was hoping we might take a trip out to see them.'

The change of subject was welcome, since he could not speak of the matter without revealing Albert's part in it. Jasper intended to make it very clear to the miller, by way of his man of business, that any promises made by Albert were his own, not the duchy's. As for the money Albert had wheedled out of the girl... He would have to think about it.

'You are talking about the abbey ruins, I presume.'

'Those, yes. Also Hardour Castle. It is quite exceptional.'

Once again, he took the lane that would lead them around the village rather than through it. He did not want to engage in meaningless chit-chat with his neighbours. Not today. 'We cannot visit both in one day. They lie in opposite directions. Which one would you prefer to visit first?'

She seemed surprised by his question, as if she had not expected him to ask for her opinion. 'The castle.' Her expression softened. 'I loved visiting the castle ruins near my home when I was a girl.'

He had lived in a castle, a nasty, cold, gloomy place. 'What did you like about it?'

A dreamy expression crossed her face. 'The romance, I suppose. The idea of knights in armour riding out on destriers to fight dragons or rescue maidens in distress.'

He choked down the urge to laugh. 'I doubt they were very pleasant fellows. I always wanted to be a knight as a lad, the moment I learned they rarely bathed more than once a month.'

She wrinkled her nose. 'You do know how to spoil an illusion, do you not?'

'And here I thought you a woman without illusions.'

She gave a small unhappy sigh. 'You are right and logic tells me that the lot of women in those days would have been far worse than they are now. But I think it does no harm to look back to a simpler time with some affection. I presume you, or someone in our party, will know the history of these particular ruins?'

'I have a sketchy idea of their background. I am sure there is a book in the library with more details. I will dig it out later today.'

'Sketching. What a good idea. I will suggest to Charity and Patience that they bring their sketchbooks along. It is always a good idea for a young lady to exhibit her artistic talents.'

Inwardly, he winced at the idea of pandering to a bunch of amateur artists. He disliked offering false praise. 'If you think they will find it entertaining, I will ask Bedwell to make sure we pack some easels.' Another distasteful thought occurred to him. 'I suppose the young ladies will also be exhibiting their musical talents at some point during their visit?'

'Yes. I am sure one evening could be set aside for musical entertainment. Miss Mitchell is a fine harpist and both sisters have very pretty voices. Perhaps one of the gentlemen will play for them.'

He would wager Lord Sherbourn knew how to play. 'I am sure we can find someone.'

'Or perhaps we could get up a play,' Amelia continued. 'The girls would enjoy that immensely.'

'Provided I do not have to play a part, I am sure it can be done.'

'The great hall would be an ideal location since it has a dais at one end. We will need to find something suitable for a small group to undertake.'

She seemed so taken with the idea he could not help but enter into the spirit of the thing and be glad she was not questioning more about the miller and his problem. 'There are several books of plays in the library that might be useful. We could look at them after dinner.'

'Nothing risqué.'

He grinned. 'Certainly nothing Nell Gwyn would have delighted in playing.'

'Trouser roles, you mean.' She made a wry face. 'I certainly would not countenance any such thing for this company, though *I* have performed them in the past.' At his quizzical glance she hastened to add, 'At school. As one of the taller girls I was always cast to play the villain.'

'Not the hero?'

'Oh, no, certainly not. The villain is always dark and unappealing while the hero is always shining fair.'

'Then it would seem I must also always play the villain.'

She frowned, looking thoughtful, as they entered the gate to the estate. 'While you are not fair as all heroes must be, it is true, I do not think anyone would cast you as a villain.'

He felt cheered by her words. Clearly, she had not taken the miller's words to heart. 'Then what role would you have me play? Surely not the hero.'

She eyed him up and down. 'The mysterious stranger, perhaps.'

'Mysterious?' Intrigued, he laughed.

'You are very good at hiding your true thoughts and feelings, I think.'

They reached the entrance to Stone Hall and the gatekeeper bowed them through the gate. 'Hardly,' he scoffed lightly as they walked their horses up the drive. 'Indeed, I believe I am an open book.'

A thoughtful expression crossed her face. 'I hope not.'

What the hell did that mean?

When they reached the stables, Amelia patted her horse's neck. 'Thank you for a most enjoyable ride, Your Grace. I will let the girls know about your suggestion of getting up a play. I know they will be delighted.'

A groom rushed forward to help her down. He dismounted and bowed. 'I wish you a pleasant afternoon, Mrs Durant. I hope you will excuse me if I do not join you. I have some estate business which requires my attention for the rest of the day and I will see you at dinner.' Business involving a letter to Albert and another to his man of business in addition to the usual pile of correspondence.

'I quite understand, Your Grace.'

Did she? There was an undertone of disapproval in her voice.

To Amelia's pleasant surprise, dinner with the Duke that evening had been most enjoyable. He had been the perfect host, making sure everyone at table had an opportunity to converse with him, and keeping the general conversation flowing when it began to lag.

Lady Mary, on the other hand, had seemed distracted as if she had weighty matters on her mind. Amelia had thought about asking the lady what troubled her, but then had decided it would be too encroaching. A glance at the Duke's genial expression led her to believe that he had noticed nothing amiss. Perhaps she was imagining the distress beneath the calm exterior Lady Mary presented to the world.

Though, now that everyone had finished their desserts and ought to be given the signal to retire to the drawing room for tea, Lady Mary was staring at her wine glass as if it contained the answer to some long-standing puzzle.

Amelia, seated next to her, leaned closer. 'Do you think His Grace would like to be left alone to enjoy his port? Or do you think he would like to join us ladies in the drawing room for tea?'

Lady Mary started as if her thoughts had indeed been very far away. 'Stone never lingers in the dining room unless he has male guests. Let us all adjourn for tea.' She looked over at the Duke, who bowed his agreement.

'Bedwell, we shall remove to the drawing room now,' she announced.

The footmen rushed forward to help the ladies with their chairs. Lady Mary took Amelia's arm. 'I recently laid my hands on a particularly nice oolong I would like you to try.'

Amelia and Lady Mary left the room together, followed by the Duke with Miss Mitchell on his arm and the rest of the guests.

The tea tray arrived almost at soon as the guests had disposed themselves on seats around the drawing room. Located in the new wing of the house, not far from the dining room, this room had clearly been designed to accommodate guests and yet be welcoming and cosy. Not at all the sort of room one could describe as ducal. It was large enough to accommodate a piano in one corner, and there were two elegant card tables ready should the guests wish to play. The night being warm, there was no fire in the grate, instead an elegant arrangement of flowers in a large crystal vase graced the hearth.

Amelia settled in a chair a little apart from the rest of the guests—after all, she was here as a chaperon. It was the Mitchell girls who were to shine in company, not herself. The tea tray was placed before Lady Mary, who undertook the ritual of pouring tea with the ease of long practice. A footman hovered nearby to deliver each delicately poured cup to its recipient.

Both girls managed their cups with the grace Amelia had come to expect from them. Mr Dobson and Lord Sherbourn, were equally at home with a cup of tea. The Duke, however, declined to partake.

Once she had sipped her tea and decided it was exactly as it should be, Lady Mary smiled. 'Miss Mitchell, we have a treat in store for you and your sister tomorrow. Provided the weather is fine, the Duke has decided we shall visit Hardour Castle. It is a local beauty spot and you are to take your pencils and paints to see if you can capture it on canvas.'

'Do we walk there?' Patience asked.

'It is too far to walk,' Jasper said. 'The ladies ride in the carriage, while the gentlemen will ride.'

'A real castle?' Charity asked. 'Or one like Papa had built in the grounds of our home.'

'It is a real castle,' the Duke said. 'Though it stands as a ruin now, a great deal of it remains intact.'

'May we go inside?' Patience said.

'You may, provided you only go in those parts that I show you are safe.'

'How exciting. I have never been inside a real castle,' Patience said.

'There won't be any ghosts, will there?' Charity asked. She sounded so hen hearted, Amelia wanted to give her a shake.

The Duke, on the other hand, seemed amused. His lips twitched slightly. 'Odd that you should ask that, Miss Mitchell. I have heard the locals say it is haunted by the spirit of the great lady who lived there before it was put to ruin by Cromwell.'

Was he trying to scare the girl? If so, he was succeeding. Charity's cheek lost some colour and she gasped and put a hand to her heart. 'I shall not go in.'

'You need not fear ghosts while I am by your side,' Lord Sherbourn said.

Instead of offering to be her champion, as he should, Jasper simply looked down his nose. 'I doubt it will come to that. She only appears at night.'

Charity looked unconvinced and turned an imploring gaze on Lord Sherbourn. To his credit the young man rose to the occasion. 'You shall not go in, if you do not wish it, and nor shall I.'

'Then it is settled,' Lady Mary announced in brisk tones. 'You shall picnic tomorrow at Hardour. Now, is anybody interested in a game of silver loo?'

'Our papa frowns on gambling,' Patience said.

'Oh, my dear,' Lady Mary said. 'We will not play for money, but for counters. But if you prefer we can play something else, like…'

'Oh, no. If no money is involved, we shall play silver loo. That is, if our dear Mrs Durant approves.'

'I see no harm in it,' Amelia said. She glanced at the Duke. 'Will you play, Your Grace?'

'I think that would make the numbers uneven, if Sherbourn intends to make up the four.'

Why was he giving in to his rival? Did he not see this was an opportunity to show Charity he could unbend enough to have a little fun? She fidgeted with her fan, wishing she could give him advice. But what could she say in company?

'May Dobson and I use your chess set, Your

Grace?' Patience asked, gesturing to the small table near the piano where chessmen lined up in perfect formation.

Jasper bowed. 'Indeed, you may.'

While Lady Mary organised the table for silver loo, Jasper stood nearby, watching the proceedings with what Amelia could only describe as a jaundiced eye.

She must have made some sort of motion, because Lady Mary glanced over sat her, and then at her nephew. 'Will you play for us, Mrs Durant?'

Amelia stiffened. She almost had the sense that this was some sort of test. Perhaps Lady Mary suspected there was something going on between her and Jasper. She went hot all over. Surely not? It was likely her own guilt making her see censure where there was none.

'I would be delighted, Lady Mary.'

Lady Mary nodded. 'You will find sheet music beneath the lid of the stool if you need it.'

It had been a long time since Amelia had played. Durant had been tone deaf and hated that anyone else should enjoy what he could not. Amelia sifted through the sheets, looking for something familiar. She did not want to stutter and stumble through something she had never tried before.

At the bottom of the pile were several pieces she knew from her childhood. These would do very well.

She set the one she knew the best on the stand and sat down.

Jasper came up to stand at her side. 'Allow me to turn the pages for you.'

His deep voice sent a shiver down her spine. She stiffened against her reaction and frowned at him. Instead of standing at her side, he should be standing with Charity, joining in the fun. Even if he was not actually playing he could make himself useful by suggesting what cards she might play in order to win.

She glanced up at him and then at the table where a good deal of laughter suggested the game was already underway. What was the matter with the man? Could he not see what was under his nose?

What could she do? One could hardly send a duke about his business.

She did the only thing she could do. She played. Each time he reached down to turn the page of music she inhaled the subtle smell of his cologne. It teased at her senses and reminded her of other times when she had breathed in that delicious scent. Heat travelled up her face and she was prayed no one would notice.

'You are a woman full of hidden talents,' he murmured in a low voice.

Her heart seemed to miss a beat at the innuendo. She smiled stiffly. 'Most ladies learn to play a musical instrument in the schoolroom.'

'Not always with such mastery, Mrs Durant.'

She finished the piece with a rousing crescendo and started to rise.

'Do not stop, my dear Mrs Durant,' Lady Mary called out. 'Your playing is delightful.'

'Thank you, Lady Mary.'

She shuffled through the other pieces and began playing an old English ballad. Without thought she began singing the words she had learned as a child.

'As I said…' Jasper leaned close and turned the page '…a woman of many talents.'

She managed not to stumble over the words, despite the heat trickling through her body.

'Your mother used to sing that song, Jasper,' Lady Mary remarked, putting down a card and glancing towards the piano. 'Do you remember?'

Amelia sensed a coldness rise within him. 'I do not.'

'Surely you must. You and she used to sing it as a duet.'

'I have no recollection of it,' he said. 'I do not sing.'

The haughtiness in his voice made it seem as if singing was beneath him.

When Amelia finished the piece, he moved away to observe Patience and Mr Dobson with little more than a bow and a nod in her direction. Amelia took it as a dismissal and rose from the piano seat.

'I win,' Charity announced, putting down the last card in her hand and gathering up a pile of markers.

'So you do,' Lady Mary said. 'Perhaps you would care to sing for us. If Mrs Durant is willing to continue playing.' She smiled indulgently. 'Since it seems I cannot persuade Jasper to add his voice to yours, Mrs Durant.'

Amelia sighed. It seemed there would be no escape for her after all. She and Charity sang several duets before the party broke up for the evening. Jasper did not speak to her again, though he did add his voice to the praise for Charity. While Amelia was pleased that he did so, he sounded quite stiff, unlike Lord Sherbourn, who was effusive in his admiration and made Charity blush delightfully.

She thought about visiting his room and giving him a few pointers on how to court the vivacious girl, but decided against it when she realised just how tempting she found the idea.

The next morning, upon his return from a meeting with his bailiff at the home of a tenant experiencing a problem with flooding, Jasper frowned to see an unknown mount in his stables. The creature's head hung low and its flanks were steaming. It had been ridden hard for some considerable distance.

'Mr Albert, sir,' the groom explained at his enquiry.

Anger rose in Jasper's gorge. He strode from the stables into the house, looking for his aunt.

He found her seated at her escritoire in her private sitting room. She looked flustered at his entry. As well she might.

'What is Albert doing here?' he said.

'Really, Jasper, is that any form of morning greeting?'

He ignored her complaint. 'He knows he is not welcome here and I doubt if he would have the temerity to turn up unless you invited him.'

His aunt stared down her nose. 'I merely mentioned that we would be here for a week or two in my letter. I certainly would not invite him without your approval.'

Jasper forced himself to calm down. 'Well, now that he is here, I will have a word with him. White informs me that his daughter very nearly succumbed to his charms a fortnight ago. He took money from the girl and her father is demanding repayment.'

The colour drained from his aunt's face. She wrung her hands together. 'Surely not? He promised me—'

His aunt, generally a sensible woman, was blind when it came to the matter of Albert. 'When will you cease being taken in by his lies?'

Her wrinkled cheeks reddened. 'How do you know it is not the girl who is lying? Girls of that sort will do anything to hide their misdeeds. And truth to tell, it is well known in the village that the miller's daughter is no better than she should be.'

Jasper ground his back teeth. She was not wrong. 'There is no smoke without a fire. I do not want him here.'

'Jasper,' his aunt said. 'His mother was a good friend to your mother. *She* would never have turned him away as you have done.'

He had never told his aunt the full compendium of Albert's misdeeds. He wasn't a tattletale, but he wished his aunt would trust him to know what was right.

'Besides,' Lady Mary continued, 'our numbers are decidedly out of balance. He will make us an even number and even you must admit he is always willing to help make a party successful.'

When he wasn't running from the bailiffs or chasing bits of muslin. This escapade with the miller's daughter was something new and even Jasper had to admit it was out of character. Albert was a charmer and a rogue, who managed to inveigle his way into polite society based on those characteristics. He did not normally go beyond the pale, however.

His aunt held out an imploring hand. 'It will only be for a week. After that, he has an invitation to shoot with one of his military friends.'

And no doubt he'd been thrown out of his lodgings for failure to pay his rent. Jasper inhaled deeply. Perhaps there was a way to handle the miller's complaint and deal with Albert's rotten behaviour once and for all. Not that Aunt Mary would be pleased with the result. But it really was time.

'He can stay, provided he promises to behave himself.'

Aunt Mary rose and stood on tiptoes to kiss his cheek. 'I knew you would come around.'

Jasper shook his head at her. 'You need to stop protecting him, Aunt. Really you do. Where is he?'

'He joined the ladies who decided to take a turn around the rose garden after breakfast, leaving me to finish my correspondence.'

Damn. He'd have to change out of his riding clothes before joining his guests.

'By the way, I assigned Albert to the blue room,' his aunt said.

The blue room was on the third floor and well away from the ladies. Perhaps his aunt did guess about more of Albert's doings than Jasper had thought. He bowed himself out and strode for his bedchamber.

By the time he was dressed and presentable, the ladies had finished their perambulations and were ensconced in the drawing room. When Jasper entered, Albert was in the middle of some gossipy story about a gentleman who had failed to observe a man painting the upper windows of a house and who had suffered the unfortunate consequences of passing under the ladder.

All of the ladies were laughing, including Mrs Durant. Even the rather dour Lord Sherbourn seemed thoroughly entertained. But that was Albert's way, wasn't it?

The moment Albert caught sight of Jasper he leaped to his feet and came forward, hand outstretched with a smile of pure delight.

The man was blond, tall and lithe. Definitely hero material—according to Mrs Durant, anyway. Jasper gritted his teeth at the falseness of that smile.

'Coz,' Albert said, taking his hand and pumping it vigorously. 'Good of you to invite me to such a charming party.'

Jasper hated that Albert insisted on calling him cousin despite they were not related. 'How are you, Albert? I was surprised to hear of your arrival. You and I must have some private time together later this afternoon.'

A shadow flickered in the depths of Albert's light blue eyes. His smile became a little stiff. 'It will be my pleasure, dear boy.'

At one point, hearing Albert refer to him as his dear boy had been a great source of pride in Jasper's young life. He'd learned the hard way that this was yet another false coin.

Albert turned to the gathered guests. 'I am told we are to set out on a picnic in a short while. The ladies have been kind enough to offer me a place in their carriage, since my horse will be far too tired to set out on another journey today.'

'I did not bring my horse,' Lord Sherbourn said with a glower. 'I had thought to ride with the ladies.'

Miss Mitchell frowned. 'Oh, dear. There is not enough room for both of you.'

For a moment, Jasper thought about scotching the notion of either of the two men riding in the carriage with the ladies and offering them horses instead. Except it did not suit his purpose.

'Mrs Durant,' he said with a smile. 'Perhaps you would consent to ride Pepper again? She is not suitable for either of these gentlemen. They are far too heavy.'

Albert gave him a mock look of horror. 'Good Lord, Jasper, I hope you are not implying I am fat.' Given his slender figure, it was clearly a jest.

The ladies laughed.

Mrs Durant looked anxious, then nodded. 'Very well, Your Grace, I will give up my place in the carriage to Mr Carling and ride Pepper. It will be my pleasure.'

'Dear lady—' Albert beamed '—you are kindness itself.

Jasper's smile was as false as Albert's.

Chapter Fourteen

The party began the one-hour journey to the Hardour ruins an hour later. While Mr Dobson, who had brought his own horse, rode alongside the carriage, no doubt intending to keep a close and jealous eye on Patience, Amelia and Jasper rode ahead. To ride behind would have left them swallowing the dust kicked up by the very fashionable barouche the Duke had provided for his lady guests.

Lady Mary had elected to remain behind at Stone Hall. Once more, it was Amelia's task to ensure the proprieties were observed. It would have been nice to have been spared this duty and simply enjoyed the day. The pleasure of riding out on Pepper caused her to wonder if her finances might stretch to a horse once she retired to the countryside. Likely they would, if the Duke offered for Charity.

Her heart dipped. What? Did she worry for Charity, or for herself? For Charity, of course. She had no intention of marrying again and did not intend to become mistress to any man, least of all a man who carelessly ignored the concerns of one of his tenants. And then there was his lack of sense when it came to courting. Someone ought to steer him in the right direction, because from her vantage point he was making a total mull of it.

After exchanging a few words about the weather and the distance as they rode off, Jasper reverted to his usual aloof silence.

'Your cousin Albert is a charming fellow,' she said, hearing laughter from the carriage behind them.

'Yes, he is, is he not?' The tone of the response was as dry as dust.

Did he not like his cousin? Did he consider him beneath his notice? 'I do not believe he was mentioned in *Debrett's*. Is he related on your mother's side? I am not familiar with the Carling name.'

'The connection is exceedingly distant.'

The ice in his tone sent a chill down her spine she tried to ignore. He was not a warm man and perhaps he did not mean to sound so cold.

'It was good of you to invite him to join us.'

'It was my aunt's doing, I can assure you.'

She frowned. 'I have the sense I have met him somewhere before.'

'Do you?'

Did he have to sound so dashed uninterested? Well, she would just ask Mr Carling if he had any recollection of a previous meeting.

She let the matter drop. She had more important concerns on her mind and it was likely this was the only chance she would have to converse with Jasper in private. 'Do you think it wise to leave Charity in the company of Lord Sherbourn quite so much?'

'Do you think I need worry about him stealing Miss Mitchell from under my nose?'

There was amusement in his tone along with incredulity. Heavens, but sometimes the man was so conceited. So sure of his lofty position. 'You may be a duke, Jasper, but Charity is an impressionable young woman and she has feelings. A young lady wishes to know she is admired by her suitor.' She had not intended to sound quite so schoolmistressish, but really, he annoyed her beyond endurance.

'I should be playing the besotted swain, then? I prefer to leave all that dramatic stuff to Lord Sherbourn. It is not exactly my style, dearest.'

Her foolish heart tumbled over at the endearment. Foolish indeed. She would *not* be lured back into his bed no matter how sweet he was to her. She forced herself back to the task at hand. 'I do not advise you follow Sherbourn's example, certainly.' She made a face. 'But you could show a little more…interest. See to her comforts and so forth. A lady likes to know she is appreciated.'

'So that is what I did wrong.'

'I beg your pardon?'

'No need. I was thinking out loud. I should not do that. My aunt tells me it is a most annoying habit.' He smiled at her and her stomach flipped over. When he smiled that particular way, there was a sweetness to his expression that make him seem like a different person, a younger man, with a spark of fun in his heart. As always, it disappeared so swiftly she wondered if she had imagined it.

They turned into a narrow sunken lane, where the hedges standing on banks that rose to the height of her horse's shoulder towered above them. He turned to look back at the carriage. She glanced back to see what had caught his attention and realised it required some considerable skill for his coachman to drive the equipage down the narrow lane and he was likely assuring himself all was well.

'I would certainly not care to attempt travelling this lane after it has rained,' she remarked.

'Nor I. The villagers are always complaining about how dreadful it is, but the owner of this land likes it this way. It deters all but the most adventurous from making the trek out to the castle and disturbing his sheep.'

Again, that dry tone. She stared at him and saw the twinkle of amusement in his eyes. 'Oh, my goodness. You are the owner.' She laughed. 'How very disobliging of you.'

'Do you think so? I can assure you my sheep are the better for it. Not to mention that I do not have to worry about some fool or other breaking a leg clambering over the wall or their neck falling out of the tower.'

'Surely not?'

'It happened. Once.' He looked grim.

'I see.'

'The castle was occupied by my family, centuries ago. I am grateful to Cromwell for its demolition.'

'Your family supported the Stuarts, then.'

'They did when it suited them.'

The lane turned a corner and the hedges gave way to a view of a forest to the left and a green hill dotted with grazing sheep rising to their right. At its crest stood a broken tower surrounded by crumbling walls. A clear blue sky arched over their heads and all the greens of summer blended to make the scene one of surprising beauty.

'How lovely,' she said. 'I had not expected anything quite so large.'

'It must have been quite a sight in its heyday.' He turned his horse and they waited for the carriage to join them.

Amelia could not help but admire the picture of the two beautiful Mitchell sisters, their complexions shaded by dainty parasols and their obvious enjoyment of the drive in the carriage.

The coachman pulled up alongside Jasper and touched his hat. Jasper dismounted and he and his cousin and the other two gentlemen helped the ladies down and unloaded the picnic baskets and blankets. They had all agreed they could manage for themselves and leave the servants to their chores at Stone Hall.

They laid the blankets beneath a large oak tree a little distant from the castle wall and set the baskets in the shade. Mr Carling immediately made himself

useful by pouring the ladies glasses of delicious and
cool lemonade from flasks packed in straw and ice.

Having refreshed themselves, the party agreed that
they would like to stretch their legs and look around
the ruins.

Jasper led the way through what at one time must
have been an imposing gate in the curtain wall and
along the overgrown track which led to the keep.
They climbed the steps and entered into the cool
of thick stone walls. Amelia shivered at the sudden
change in temperature.

Light pierced the gloom from windows and from
an enormous jagged hole on the other side of what
must have been the great hall.

'The ground floor is perfectly safe, as are the two
staircases on the north side.' Stone's voice echoed
hollowly, seeming to come from several directions
at once. 'The south side where the breach occurred
cannot be trusted. With that in mind, wander where
you will, but please do not go alone.'

Amelia looked about her. 'How cold this place
must have been in winter.'

'Freezing, I should think,' Charity said and shivered. 'I am glad we do not live in castles any more.'

Jasper raised a brow. 'Some of us still do live in
castles.'

Charity flushed. 'Oh, I am sure yours must be all
warm and cosy with all modern conveniences, Not
at all like this one.'

His expression became bland. 'It has been somewhat modernised over the years, but there are still

many cold and draughty corners, I am afraid. To be honest, I would not describe it as cosy or convenient. It is, however, very grand.'

Was he trying to frighten Charity, or was he simply too obtuse to see the dismay his words had caused.

'Come and see the size of this fireplace,' Lord Sherbourn called out. 'There is room for three or four people to stand within.'

Charity hastened towards him.

'Did you have to make your home sound so unappealing?' Amelia said sotto voce, afraid that her words would carry in the echoing space.

'I only speak the truth,' he replied calmly. 'Come, let me show you what we think must have been the ladies' bower. It is up this staircase.'

Amelia glanced over at the Mitchell girls standing in the hearth and exclaiming in wonder at its size. They would be safe enough for a moment or two.

'Very well.' It really was time she explained a few things to Jasper and not by way of gentle hints, either. They didn't seem to work.

Jasper had not visited Hardour since he was a lad, before his parents died. Indeed, now he thought about it, he recalled it had been their last family outing. His father had spoken of the past glories of the Warren family and how they had survived all of the turbulent periods of Britain's history.

Jasper had been fascinated, wishing he had been born in the time of knights and jousts. His father had laughed and said he had done the same as a boy, but knew better now.

It had been a good day.

A day he had deliberately not recalled in years. He always found those recollections too painful to bear. Today he felt only warmth.

In the centre of the small room, Amelia slowly turned around as she looked about her. So slender. So elegant. So full of womanly poise. So unlike the innocent naive Miss Mitchell. He wanted to take her in his arms and kiss her silly. Fortunately, he knew better than to rush his fences.

'This would have been where the women of the castle gathered to sew and weave and gossip under the watchful eye of their lady,' she said. 'The light from this window would have been ideal.'

She sat on the window ledge as if to test her theory. 'Oh, my word. One can see for miles.'

'A way of preventing an enemy from making a surprise attack.'

'Or for the lady of the house to see her lord on his way home and make the necessary preparations. If I remember my history correctly, she would order a tub to be sent up and bathe her husband.'

His groin tightened. 'Now there is an intriguing idea.'

'It is, isn't it?' She flushed and turned her gaze out of the window. 'Goodness, I did not intend to say that out loud.'

He laughed. 'You may say whatever pleases you. I will not judge. For a widow you are a shy little thing.'

'Me shy?' She shook her head and gazed at him. 'It think not. I would hardly be a successful matchmaker if I was shy.'

'Modest, then.'

Her lips tightened. 'Perhaps.'

'You know,' he said, wanting to tease her and see her blush again, 'in addition to washing her husband a lady of the castle would also be expected to assist his knights at their bath.'

A crease formed between her brows. 'Wouldn't that be a little awkward?'

He heard amusement in her voice. 'It might be, depending on the husband.' He frowned. 'If it were me, I would have someone else take on the task. Preferably a matron with a quiver full of children and the figure to prove it.'

She laughed. 'I rather think that would be seen as the lady shirking her duty.'

'As long as she bathed me, the rest of them could go hang.'

'You would be a jealous husband, then.'

'I cannot see myself sharing my wife in any way, shape or form.'

'Yet you do not seem to mind that Charity spends much of her time with Sherbourn.'

'I explained that.'

'I do not believe it is working. They are closer than ever. I really think you need to exert yourself. Charm her. Make her feel treasured and admired.'

'I am not a charming man.'

'You can be, if you wish. Pay her a compliment

now and then. Gift her with a bouquet occasionally. Single her out and walk with her. Let her get to know you as a person, rather than merely be acquainted with the Duke.'

'Are they not one and the same?' Damnation. Now he was angling for a compliment from her. 'Never mind. Did you know you have the most astonishingly lovely eyes I have ever seen?'

She blinked. Her expression softened. 'I—thank you.' She inhaled a quick breath. 'You see, you can do it if you try.'

He took her gloved hand in his and stroked the back of it with his thumb. Even with the two layers of fabric between them, his touch raised little bumps in the space between her gloves and her short sleeves. 'Sometimes.'

She shivered. 'We really should be going down. Then you can try these wiles of yours on Miss Mitchell. Talk to her in that tone of voice, look at her that way and she is sure to swoon at your feet.'

He would prefer that Amelia swoon at his feet. But not here. Not in this draughty old ruin.

He helped her rise from the stone window seat and gazed down at her. He lowered his face to hers at the same moment she lifted her chin and her lips parted. Before she could speak, he kissed her.

For an instance she relaxed in his arms and kissed him back with a fierce hunger. A kiss so passionate, heat rushed through his body. He pulled her tight against him, loving the feel of her slender back beneath his palms. The light summer fabric of her gown allowed him to feel every contour of her lithe body.

She pushed against his chest and he stepped back, inhaling a deep calming breath. 'Jasper. You must not. Good heavens, what if someone saw? Charity would never forgive you.'

Now there was a thought.

'You enjoyed that as much as I did.'

Pink stained her exotic cheekbones. 'I won't deny it. But it must never happen again. I will have your word as a gentleman.'

He cast his gaze up at the ceiling and then back at her, weighing his words carefully. 'It will not happen again, unless you ask.'

'Good,' she said. 'Come, let us go down before we are missed and someone comes searching.'

'Let me go ahead. The stairs are treacherous.'

She followed him down the winding staircase. Sadly, not once did she stumble and give him the opportunity to play the good knight.

Knowing Jasper preceded her, prepared to catch her should she misstep, was extraordinarily comforting. It had been years since anyone had cared what happened to her. Her husband certainly had not, or he would have provided for her welfare before he went and got himself killed. Jasper would never do that to his wife. He took his responsibilities seriously. Unfortunately, he also took himself too seriously. To him, consequence was everything. Which was why she still did not quite understand why he was interested in Charity.

But he was interested in her and it was up to Amelia to bring about their union.

A pain seized her heart. Jealousy? Surely not?

Why on earth had she gone off with him alone? His allure ripped at the defences she'd erected around her deeper emotions. If he used even a fraction of his charm on Charity, the girl would fall into his arms as easily as Amelia had.

Because she was letting her heart rule her head. It was quite obvious Stone was amusing himself before settling down to business and making an offer to the woman who would become his wife. It was ridiculous of her to pine after him when she never wanted to be under a man's thumb ever again. Surely she had learned that lesson.

After all, she wanted to live out her days doing exactly what she pleased.

At the bottom of the stairs, they discovered that the rest of the party had disappeared.

'Where did they go?'

He glanced through the window. 'Outside.'

They wandered out into the sunshine. Patience had set up her easel and Mr Dobson was stretched out on the grass in front of her, clearly posing for a portrait. Charity was giggling at something Mr Carling was saying, while he leaned casually on her folded easel. Amelia frowned. Mr Carling seemed almost a little too familiar, standing too close and occasionally touching Charity's arm.

'Why don't you take Charity to a spot where there is a particularly fine view while I get to know Mr Carling a little better?' Amelia said to Jasper.

He sighed. 'Very well. If that is your wish.'

When they joined the other two, he gave Charity a beaming smile. 'May I suggest the perfect place to set up your easel, Miss Mitchell?' he said.

Carling stiffened, then gave his cousin a mock glare. 'I am about to do that, Coz. I was telling Miss Mitchell that the best view to be had was from the summerhouse your father built. From there she will have a spectacular view of the county and be shaded from the sun.'

'The summerhouse,' Jasper scoffed. 'I expect it is full of dust and spiders after all this time.'

Miss Mitchell made a sound of dismay.

Albert glared at him.

He grinned cheerfully. 'I know of a spot where you can include the ruins in your view. Come, I will show you.' He took hold of the easel, causing Carling to stagger, and tucked it under his arm.

Anger flashed across Carling's face, swiftly replaced by an easy smile. 'It is rare for you to be so enthusiastic about anything, my dear Coz.'

'Do you think so, Carling?'

Charity looked at Amelia, who nodded. 'I think your papa would be interested in a view of the castle, don't you?' She looked around. 'Where is Lord Sherbourn?'

Charity's mouth tightened. 'I could not say.'

Carling chuckled. 'The young man took offence

when I suggested his idea of where Miss Mitchell should set up her easel was ridiculous.'

That sounded like Lord Sherbourn.

'I gather you are familiar with the ruins, Mr Carling,' Amelia said. 'Perhaps you would do me the honour of providing me with some of the history of the place.'

His eyes narrowed a fraction. He glanced swiftly at his cousin who was walking Charity to a spot at the edge of the woods. He gave Amelia a droll look. 'Trying to get my cousin up to scratch, are you, Mrs Durant?'

'It is why we came to Stone Hall.'

His eyebrows shot up. 'Such directness. How very charming.' He did not sound in the least bit charmed. Nevertheless, he took her arm and they walked towards what must have been an outer wall. He pointed to the pile of rubble. 'This is where Cromwellian forces broke through. After that they turned their cannon on the keep itself. The lord of the day was a pragmatic chap, apparently, and hoisted the white flag, but Cromwell's orders were to bring down the castle. And so they did.'

He turned and glanced up at where Jasper had set up Charity's easel and now sprawled beside her on the grass with all the grace of a predatory beast.

'They make a lovely couple do they not?' she said. 'Her so beautiful and fair and him so handsome and honourable.'

He gave her a dark look. 'It would appear so.'

'You sound doubtful.'

He grimaced. 'My word, Mrs Durant, you are a perspicacious woman.'

Not all gentlemen appreciated a woman who could read between the lines. 'What gives you cause for concern?'

He turned and gazed out over the countryside to the east of the tower. 'You can see the spire of Saint Jude's from here. Cromwell's men destroyed all its statues and adornments.'

'You changed the subject, Mr Carling.'

'I should not have spoken. It is not my place to have an opinion.'

Should she leave well enough alone? But what if there were things he knew about Jasper that others did not? She quite often had the feeling he was keeping his true self hidden. 'But you did so. And now I would like to know the basis for your doubts.'

'Aunt Mary says we must make allowances for my cousin,' he said softly. 'After all, his childhood was marred by his parents' death. Before that dreadful event, he and I were like brothers. Or I thought we were. When he inherited the title, he changed. He began to view all around him as lesser mortals hardly worthy of his notice.'

She remembered the hurt of her own experience. 'You included, I suppose. That must have caused you pain.'

He bowed slightly. 'Indeed. Therefore...' He hesitated.

'Go on. I prefer frank speaking.'

He took a deep breath. 'I do wonder at his motives

in pursuing a bride so far beneath him when he despises the lower classes.'

There, her own doubts echoed by someone who knew him much better than she. And yet instinctively she felt a desire to defend. 'While I have wondered the same thing, I do know he is an honourable man. I am sure any wife of his would be treated with the utmost respect.'

His expression hardened. 'Do you think so, indeed? When he treats his own relations with such disdain?'

She gasped. 'I beg your pardon.'

He turned to face her, his expression serious. 'Are you sure you wish to know?'

'I do,' she said firmly, though her heart beat wildly.

'Well, you see how he treats me, do you not? Oh, I will admit that outwardly he is polite to a fault, but in truth time and again he has dashed all my hopes quite deliberately. *I* should have inherited Stone Hall. It is one of the few ducal properties not covered by the entail. His father always promised it would be mine. Sadly, his father died unexpectedly, without a will.' He frowned. 'Or at least, no will was located.' He shook his head. 'It was most unlike the last Duke to be so careless.'

'You are not suggesting that His Grace had something to do with the will not being found?'

He gave a bitter laugh and brushed a lock of hair out of his eyes. 'Jasper is a duke, no one dares take my word over his. Whatever the case, Jasper refused to honour his father's wishes, despite knowing them.'

She gazed at him. 'If this is true, I am shocked. Indeed, it is hard for me to believe—'

He gave a hard laugh. 'Far more shocking was his refusal to write a reference when I was offered a government position. Indeed, I believe he did quite the opposite— I really should not say more.'

This was unsettling to say the least. If a man would behave so badly to a relation, who it seemed had done nothing to cause him harm, how would he treat a wife if she made any sort of misstep?

No one was perfect. Yet, while she knew Jasper to be proud, she had not seen him as vindictive. Indeed, he had been nothing but kindness to her and to the Mitchell girls. Was he playing some kind of game?

'Why would he go to such lengths to spoil your future?'

'I know not, Mrs Durant. Unless he was jealous of his father's fondness for me. But you will not speak of this. Nor think of it again, I implore you. I should have said nothing. My Aunt Mary does her best to intercede for me and I hope that one day she will be successful in getting me my rightful inheritance. Until then, I must be at my cousin's beck and call.'

'I do not understand?'

'Why, you do not think I came here of my own accord, do you? To this place which holds so many memories of dashed hopes? No. I am here because Jasper demanded my presence. The small allowance he grants me depends on my observing his wishes.'

A cold space opened in the pit of her stomach. The man described by Mr Carling, was not the sort of husband she would wish on any woman. Always, she had promised herself that she would not promote a match, if she was not certain the parties would be compatible. Once she had got to know Jasper her earlier doubts had seemed unreasonable. Now, they once more reared their ugly heads.

Somehow she must extricate Charity from what threatened to be a disastrous match.

Watching Albert with Amelia while he was forced to entertain Miss Mitchell was annoying in the extreme. Who knew what lures Albert was throwing out? But surely the sensible and intelligent Amelia would see right through him?

Yet he had a bad feeling in his gut.

'What do you think, Stone?' Charity said after working away at her sketch for a good half-hour or more.

He inspected the canvas that she turned towards him. The drawing of the ruins, all dark and foreboding, was surprisingly good. 'I think you have a talent for drawing, Miss Mitchell.'

She blushed. 'You are very kind.'

'Not at all. I speak the truth. Not that I would count myself an expert, but you have captured the mysterious essence of the old keep. I see you have chosen to omit the distant countryside. I wonder if it would not serve as a good juxtaposition to the darkness of the ruin.'

She smiled sweetly. 'Oh, yes, I see what you mean.

I will do so at once.' Head bent over the drawing, she set to work.

She was a nice young lady. Sweet. Pretty. And far too compliant to be interesting. Unlike Amelia, who never failed to give her own opinion. Or was it that Miss Mitchell was intimidated by his title? Either way, he felt uncomfortable.

Once more he turned his gaze down the hill to see Mrs Durant walking towards them. He rose and went to meet her. As he got closer he could see she looked troubled. What had Albert said? 'Is something wrong?'

She glanced at Charity. 'I think I need a few words with you alone.' She drew close to Charity and looked at her work. 'Oh, that is excellent. Why don't you head down to the picnic? I am sure you must be getting hungry. His Grace and I will bring your easel and so on.'

'I am hungry,' Charity said. 'I will go on ahead and set out the food.'

Always so obliging. Jasper shook his head at his uncharitable thought and went to help Amelia. She shot him an impatient glance when he took the sketchbook from her hand and tucked it inside Charity's portfolio.

Once Charity was out of earshot he moved to stand in front of her. 'What is it that has you troubled, Amelia?'

'I would like to request that you withdraw from the lists. I do not think you and Charity will suit.'

Her words struck like a blow to the solar plexus.

'What has brought this about?' he asked, but he could only guess it has something to do with her conversation with Albert. He should have known better than to have left the two of them together.

'I do not think she is the right sort of girl for you. Her background is not what a duke would expect in a wife. It is my belief neither of you will be happy.'

Did she care about his happiness or only Charity's? 'What grounds do you have for making such an assumption, Mrs Durant?'

'Your Grace, after what I heard about your treatment of Albert, there is no other conclusion I can draw.'

He felt as if the breath had been knocked out of his body. 'My treatment of Albert Carling?' He could not keep the incredulity out of his voice. 'Am I to know of what I am accused?'

'Do you deny that you have refused him his rightful inheritance and ruined his chances of decent employment?'

Ice filled his veins. He had thought she knew him better than to believe such nonsense. Clearly, he was wrong. He picked up the easel and the box of drawing materials. 'Then there is no more to be said. Perhaps you would be good enough to carry Miss Mitchell's portfolio.'

He marched down the hill, not caring if she followed or not. Seeing nothing, feeling nothing. Happiness. What a stupid word.

When they arrived at the picnic spot, they found Charity sitting on the blanket unpacking the hampers.

'Where is everyone?' Amelia asked. Her voice sounded strained.

'Mr Dobson was here when I arrived and he went to tell Lord Sherbourn we plan to eat now. Mr Carling took Patience to see the Roman ruins that lie a little way up the hill. He was explaining how this sight had been used as a fort for centuries and of course Patience had to see for herself. They won't be long.'

He and Amelia helped her to lay out the picnic. And still the others did not return.

Jasper's stomach churned. 'Surely they should be back by now?'

'I will ring the bell,' Amelia said. 'That should bring them.'

It brought Dobson and Lord Sherbourn, who smiled somewhat shyly at Charity. Damn, but the boy wore his heart on his sleeve. 'I found the best thing ever,' he said. 'A punt. We can go for a boat ride on the lake after we eat.'

'Did you see Patience, Mr Dobson?' Amelia asked.

The young man shook his head. 'She said she was perfectly content to remain where she was while I went in search of Sherbourn.'

Four pairs of eyes turned to Lord Sherbourn. He shook his head, looking worried and a little shamefaced. 'I was on my way back here when I ran into Dobson. I saw no one else.'

Dobson nodded.

'Surely they must have heard the bell?' Amelia said. 'Could something have happened to them?'

'I expect they are on their way,' Sherbourn said.

A cold feeling trickled through Jasper's veins. 'We need to mount a search. We will go in groups. We do not want anyone else going missing. Mrs Durant, I and Miss Mitchell will head for the ruins you spoke of. Sherbourn and Dobson, you go north-west. Call out as you go. If you do not find them after fifteen minutes, return here and we will set out in another direction.'

'How can we let each other know if we do find them?'

'Return here and ring the bell,' Jasper said.

Everyone's expressions had become serious, Dobson's particularly. 'I should not have left her alone.'

Amelia placed a comforting hand on his shoulder. 'She was not alone. And she is not. She is with Mr Carling.'

Jasper wished that notion made him feel better, not worse. Carling always had money troubles. And Miss Patience was just as much an heiress as her sister... He cut the thought off. His aunt always accused him of thinking the worst of Albert, but past experience had taught him not to trust the man. Try as he might to think otherwise, he very much feared there would not be an innocent explanation for this disappearance.

Chapter Fifteen

Amelia sensed that as calm as Jasper seemed, he was worried. There was something he was not saying, no doubt because he wanted to spare her and Charity's feelings. Or was it because he did not like Mr Carling? Had Jasper truly been jealous of his father's fondness for the man?

As they walked, they called out for Patience and Mr Carling.

'I expect Patience is engrossed in some obscure piece of nature or picking up shards of Roman pots and has forgotten all about us,' Charity said.

'I am sure that is all it is.' Jasper didn't sound convinced.

'How like her to keep us all waiting for our luncheon.' She chuckled. 'I hope she is not plaguing poor Mr Carling to death with all her questions.'

A second later, she gave a sharp cry.

Amelia dashed to her side when she saw her sprawled on the ground.

Jasper knelt beside her. 'What is it? Are you hurt?'

His concern seemed so genuine, it was hard to believe he had not a scrap of feeling for his fellow man.

'Are you all right?' Amelia asked.

'I caught my foot in a root and twisted my ankle. It is nothing. Let us go on.' She rose with Jasper's help, took a step and gasped with pain.

'You are not going anywhere on a twisted ankle,' Jasper said grimly.

'Oh, but we must find Patience,' Charity said. 'I want to help.'

'I will carry you back to the blanket and you watch from there. Ring the bell to let us know they have returned so we do not search needlessly.'

'That would be a big help,' Amelia said. 'I was wondering what they would think if they came back and found us all gone.'

Charity nodded. 'Very well.'

Jasper swung her up in his arms. Charity giggled. 'My goodness, you are strong.'

Dash it, the girl was looking at him with admiration in her gaze. A stab of jealousy pierced Amelia's heart. Good heavens, what was she thinking? This was what she had wanted—Jasper to play the knight errant for Charity. But that was before Mr Carling had made her decide he was unsuitable for the girl. The urge to warn Charity to have nothing to do with him almost made her speak out.

Now was not the time.

She followed in Jasper's wake as he carried Charity back to the oak tree and set her on the blanket. He handed her the bell. 'Ring it as hard as you can if our missing couple returns.'

Amelia looked around, 'Your Grace, what became of your coachman and the carriage?'

'He returned to the bottom of the hill to water the horse and find some shade.'

'Do you think he might have seen anything of Mr Carling and Patience? Shall we ask him if they passed him on the way to look at something else?'

Jasper looked towards the woods and then turned his head to consider the lane winding down the hill away from the ruins.

'Yes, but first I must put a compress on Miss Mitchell's ankle.'

'Do not trouble about me,' Charity said. 'Continue the search.' She ripped her handkerchief in half and pulled one of the bottles of water out of its nest of ice and straw. 'I can put on my own compress. Go. You, too, Mrs Durant. Two pairs of eyes are better than one.'

'If you are sure,' Amelia said.

'I most certainly am. I want Patience found. She, too, may have fallen and is now hurt.' She sounded so anxious, Amelia made no further demur, but with Jasper firmly holding her arm they hurried down the hill.

They reached the stream that ran alongside the road and saw no sign of anyone at all.

The sound of rustling in the bushes caught their attention.

'Walters?' Jasper said.

A moan met their ears. Then the large man rose

up from a patch of long grass. 'Your Grace. What happened?'

'I was going to ask you the same thing,' Jasper said. 'Where is the barouche?'

The man glanced around with a hazy expression. 'Gone. And the horses, too.'

'Did you see Mr Carling?'

'Ah, that be it. Mr Carling and one of the pretty ladies. They came walking this way. The young lady looked none too happy. Well, I'll be—' He coloured and winced. 'Mr Carling hit me on the noggin, so he did, and the young lady screamed and that was it. I woke up to see you and this lady.'

Amelia was staring at him in horror. 'Mr Carling attacked you? To what purpose?'

'I assume he wanted the carriage,' Jasper said in dry tones. 'It seems he has run off with Patience.'

'Why on earth would he do that?'

'Ah, but you see I left him with no option since Miss Charity was with me.'

She frowned. 'Surely not.' Could she really have read the situation so incredibly poorly?

Jasper looked a little bitter. 'Mr Carling is no doubt in debt up to his ears again.'

'But—' Her stomach fell away. She stared at him in horror. 'Oh, no!'

The blinkers fell away from her eyes. Mr Carling was a wretch who had used his charm to vilify Jasper. 'Oh, I am sorry for ever believing a word he said. I would never have left him with Patience—' She had left him there to take Jasper to task. She felt dreadful.

Jasper's lips thinned. 'I should have guessed he was up to something when he showed up here uninvited and unannounced.'

'He said you demanded his presence and that he had to do exactly what you asked or you would cut of the niggardly allowance you provide.'

'I provide no allowance,' he snarled. 'I gave him a princely sum and he squandered it in less than a year and I refused to support him further. But we waste time, Mrs Durant. I need to set out in pursuit.'

What had she done? She had believed a dastardly rogue when she should have known better. 'I owe you an apology, Your Grace.'

He stared down his nose and smiled grimly. 'There are more important matters to hand, Mrs Durant.' He whistled. A horse whickered from somewhere nearby and a few moments later his big bay came trotting out of the undergrowth with Pepper close on his heels.

He patted his horse's neck. 'I did not suppose you would have gone far, old chap,' he said fondly to the horse. 'You and I have a gallop in our future.'

He picked up his saddle from the ground and began tacking up.

'I'm going with you,' Amelia said. 'Patience will need a friendly female face when we catch up to them.'

For a moment, she thought he would refuse, then he gave a terse nod.

Walters helped her saddle Pepper and soon they were ready to go. 'Should we let the others know what is happening?'

'Not until we have Miss Patience back safe and sound.' They set off down the lane. 'Fortunately, there is no other direction they can go but back to the main road. Let us hope we can catch them up before they get there.'

He set his heels to his horse and pushed his horse into a gallop.

Amelia followed suit.

Jasper could scarcely contain his fury. He did not know who he was more angry at: Albert for this dastardly act of cowardice or Amelia for believing the man's lies. Charm. It was the currency women cared about. Truth, honesty and honour stood for nothing if a man did not have an easy smile and a ready address.

It seemed as if any hopes he had of finding happiness were doomed to failure. To hell with it.

He glanced back. Amelia and Pepper were trailing since Riptide was setting a blistering pace. He slowed a little, gritting his teeth at the delay. He was determined Albert would not achieve his goal of ruining Miss Patience. He had no illusion that Albert wanted to marry the girl. He would merely want money to keep his silence. The cur.

They came around the next bend to a woeful sight.

His barouche was jammed hard up against the bank, Albert was belabouring his horses, trying to free the wheels, and Miss Patience stood alongside with her hands on her hips.

She glanced up at the sound of the horses' hooves and when she saw who it was coming along she ran to meet them. Jasper swung down off his horse and helped Amelia to dismount. Patience dissolved into tears and ran into her arms.

'Thank goodness you came,' she said, sobbing into Amelia's shoulder. 'He said I would be ruined in the eyes of the world and I would have to marry him, because dear Harold would never want me after this.'

'Hush, hush,' Amelia said.

Jasper heard her talking to the girl in low soothing tones as he approached Albert, who, looking hot and sweaty, had climbed down from the driver's seat and was now standing with his arms folded.

'Well, this is a pretty mess,' Jasper said. 'You always were cow-handed when it came to driving a team.'

'Perhaps I would not be, if I had more opportunity to practice. You had your own phaeton, I had nothing but—'

'Enough.' Jasper put up a hand. 'What the devil do you think you are doing, running off with Miss Patience is such a havey-cavey way?' He waited with mild curiosity as to what sort of ridiculous excuse he would make up.

'It was all her fault. She was batting her eyes at me and...' he raised his voice so the women could hear '...telling me how romantic it would be to run off to Gretna Green.'

'I didn't want to run off with you, you idiot,' Patience shouted back. 'I love Dobson. You said you had arranged for him and me to go.'

He glared at her. 'Well, I didn't. You ran off with

me. And if you don't watch what you say, your reputation will be ruined and no one will want you.'

'No, she did not run off with you,' Amelia said calmly. 'Patience and I came for a drive after you bragged how well you could handle a team. And look how it turned out. I shall delight in telling everyone how you ran the horses off a perfectly straight road into a bank.'

'Me!' Albert went red in the face. 'She pulled on the reins.'

'Clever girl,' Amelia said.

Patience raised her tearstained face and giggled. 'You should have seen his face. He had no idea what to do.'

'We could have been killed,' Albert grumbled.

'I suggest you take yourself off,' Jasper said. 'Even across country, is a long walk back to Stone Hall and you will want to get there before nightfall so you can collect your horse and leave.'

'Walk?' Albert said.

'Be glad I don't call the magistrate and have you arrested.'

Albert's handsome face changed as he sneered, 'You wouldn't dare. On what charges? Running off with a girl who is no better than she should be.'

Jasper planted him a facer.

'Bravo,' Amelia and Patience said in unison as Albert, recumbent in the dust, stared up at him in astonishment.

Jasper rubbed at his knuckles which no doubt would be bruised, despite his leather gloves. 'You do not know how long I have wanted to do that, Albert. Now start walking. And do not dare set foot inside any one of my houses. Take your horse and leave Stone Hall immediately. If you do not, then I will see you leg-shackled to White's daughter, because I gather she is another of your victims.'

Albert glared at him. Pushed to his feet with a groan. When he saw not a scrap of sympathy from any of the onlookers, he picked up his hat and dusted it off. 'White's girl should have known better. Besides, she changed her mind at the last. A complete waste of time.'

'You are no gentleman and from here on in I shall tell everyone the truth. You are no relative of mine. What is more, if you do not start walking I will close your mouth with my fist.'

Albert offered a wheedling smile, but there was panic in his eyes. He knew very well his acceptance in society rested in Jasper's hands. 'Coz, you would not be so shabby.'

Jasper gave him an implacable stare. Nothing Aunt Mary could say after this would change his mind.

Albert glared at Patience. 'You will pay for this.'

'Do not think about it, Albert, if you want an allowance. I will provide one for Aunt Mary's sake. If you cross me in this, then consider it gone.'

'Damn you, Stone.' He shambled away.

Drawing in a steadying breath to calm his anger, Jasper went to the horses' heads, got them calmed down and gently extricated them from the bank. 'I will drive you and Miss Patience, Mrs Durant. We will tie our horses on behind. We need to get back as soon as possible, because I imagine the others are getting very worried with not two of us gone without a word, but four.'

'Perhaps if we are quick, no one will notice our absence at all,' Amelia said.

'I do not think we need worry about their discretion. Every member of our party will support Miss Patience. And I can assure you, Albert is an utter coward. He will say nothing.' He could not help the bitterness in his voice.

Amelia leaned forward and touched his arm. 'Thank you for your help.'

He turned and caught the stricken expression on her face. He hardened his heart against that look. She was another woman who had seen only his title and power. She clearly knew nothing of his character.

In the back of the barouche, Amelia felt Jasper's withdrawal like a chill in her bones. She knew now her accusations had been unjustified. That Carling had lied. She felt terrible. Worse was the feeling she had let Jasper down.

But there was nothing she could say, not at this moment. Her stomach sank. He was a proud man, perhaps he would never forgive her. Nor did she deserve that he should.

She put her arm around Patience. Despite the girl's bravery, she was trembling. 'All is well, my dear.'

'Oh, I know. And I am terribly grateful to you and

His Grace, but what will Dobson say? Perhaps he will think it my fault, like Mr Carling said.'

'If he loves you, which I know he does, he will believe in your innocence. The poor man was beside himself when he thought you were lost in the woods. Never fear, he will be delighted to have you back safe and sound.'

The words rang hollow in her ears. Deep in her heart, she had known she was falling for Jasper, so how could she have believed all those dreadful things Carling had said?

Jasper soon had them bowling along the lane back the way they had come. Walters was waiting for them at the bottom of the hill. As were all the members of their party.

'Oh, dear,' Amelia said. 'I suppose there is no way of keeping our little adventure a secret.' She frowned. 'What on earth is Lord Sherbourn doing?'

He was sitting on the grass with Charity on his lap and they were kissing.

Amelia turned her gaze to Jasper, whose face was completely expressionless. Was he hurt by this also? Had he cared for Charity more than she had supposed? Her heart ached for him, but even so she could not help feeling glad for Charity. The heiress would marry the heir to an earldom for love.

Even if they were a foolish pair.

Charity scrambled to her feet and Patience jumped down into her arms when the carriage came to a stop.

'Oh, my dear, I was so worried,' Charity said. She

cast a shy glance at Jasper. 'But I knew if anyone could save you, it would be His Grace.' She blushed when Lord Sherbourn pulled her tight against his side. 'But, you see, I love Sherbourn. He asked me to marry him and I said yes.'

Goodness, things had moved fast.

Mr Dobson pulled Patience away from Charity and ran his hands over her shoulders and down her arms. 'Did he hurt you? If so, he will meet me on the field of honour. I'll—'

'Nothing happened,' Patience said.

Jasper cast a wry look at Charity and Sherbourn. 'A great deal has happened, it seems. But Miss Patience dealt with Carling by causing him to run off the road.'

'And His Grace handed him a very wisty caster,' Patience exclaimed. 'You would have been impressed, Harold.'

Everyone stared at her, mouths agape.

'What?' she asked.

'My dear. Your language,' Charity said.

'Balderdash,' Patience said. 'It was.'

'I am sure it was,' Mr Dobson said fondly. 'His Grace is well known for having a handy right.'

Everyone laughed.

Including Jasper.

'I think it is time we called an end to this outing and returned to Stone Hall,' Jasper said. 'Walters, are you up to driving after that blow the head, or shall I take the reins?'

'I be fine, Your Grace,' Walters said. 'I'm just happy

no harm came to these beauties.' He gave each horse a loving stroke down its nose. 'Mr Albert ain't never been a dab hand with the ribbons like Your Grace.'

'I think it would be better if we did not mention Mr Albert's mischief here today, don't you?' Jasper said.

Walters frowned, then nodded. 'Mum's the word, Your Grace. Mum's the word indeed.'

The two young couples sat together in the barouche.

Amelia went to Pepper, waiting for Jasper to assist her into the saddle.

He dutifully came to her side. 'Are you sure you can manage yet another ride so soon after our gallop.'

This display of kindness after all she had done brought a lump to her throat. She was going to miss him. Oh, how could she have misjudged him so badly?

No! She would not cry. She drew in a deep steadying breath. 'Yes. I am perfectly fine, thank you.'

He bent and tossed her up into the saddle, then went to see Dobson's horse safely tied to the back of the barouche, before mounting up.

They walked the horses down the lane, with her on one side of the carriage and him on the other, making sure the proprieties among the young people were observed.

They arrived at Stone Hall without running across Mr Carling, for which small mercy Amelia was very grateful. She did not know how she would have faced the man and his smirking smile.

She accompanied Charity and Patience into the house to change for dinner, while the gentlemen arranged to go for a drink in His Grace's study, before they did the same.

When Lady Mary greeted them as they entered, the older woman looked tired and sad, 'Would you like me to have tea trays sent up to your rooms?'

'Yes, please,' all three of them chorused.

'Would it be possible to send along some biscuits?' Patience asked. 'I am famished and sadly we did not have a chance to eat any of the food sent along for the picnic.'

Lady Mary smiled tightly. 'Indeed. I will ask Cook to send up some sustenance.'

Having seen the girls safely to their rooms, Amelia collapsed in the armchair in hers, looking forward to a cup of tea.

A scratch at the door was a welcome sound. She was surprised when Lady Mary carried in the tray and jumped up.

'Do not get up,' Lady Mary said. She set down a tray containing tea for two and an assortment of breads, cheeses and *petit fours*. Her shoulders slumped. 'I must apologise for Albert's awful behaviour. He came and confessed the whole. Or rather his side of it. I guessed the rest and Stone confirmed my fears. He is beyond the pale. I can no longer find it in my heart to stand by him. When I informed him of my decision, he treated me to a tirade of vituperation I have never encountered in my life. I have been a blind fool where that fellow is concerned.'

She looked wearied to the bone. Amelia offered her a seat. 'I, too, was taken in by him.' His accusations fitted in so well with her own prejudices, it was as if he had sensed them. She had been an utter fool. 'I think it best if we say no more about it.'

'You are very generous, Mrs Durant. I am not sure I would be so kind if I were in your place.'

'Fortunately, we found Patience in time. I do think it is best if Stone and Mr Carling do not cross paths in the near future.' Any more than she would cross paths with Jasper after this. He was a good, kind and generous man who did all he could for those he cared for. He deserved happiness. She hoped with every fibre of her being that one day he would find it.

They drank their tea in silence, each lost in her own regrets.

Chapter Sixteen

At dinner, Jasper could not help but notice how absolutely lovely Amelia looked in a gown of palest green. Clearly, she was doing her best to hold up her end of the conversation, but her smiles were forced. No doubt she was anxious to depart, now it was clear Charity was not going to be marrying a duke.

Bitterness rose in his gullet. How could he have been so blind as to think Amelia was different to all the other women he'd met over the years, women who saw only his title and his power? Well, Albert Carling had done him a favour or he might have made a huge mistake where Amelia was concerned.

Aunt Mary had not joined them for dinner, but pleaded a headache after apologising profusely for her mistaken trust in Albert all these years. He could not blame her for her loyalty to the man, knowing that she had always stood loyal to him, too. He was actually sorry she'd had to finally learn the truth about Albert.

His other guests oozed happiness and were clearly

too involved in each other to notice Jasper and Amelia's silence.

Jasper could only feel satisfied that his plan of inviting the four young people to Stone Hall had paid off handsomely. The rest of his plan had come to naught. He shut off the sense of loss that threatened to overwhelm him. He'd been dealing with loss for years. What was another?

When dessert was removed, he smiled genially. 'Ladies and gentlemen, it has been a pleasure having you here at Stone Hall, but I believe that after today's events, circumstances have changed, so much so that tomorrow you should return to London.'

They all looked relieved at his words.

'I for one would like to have an audience with Patience's papa at the earliest opportunity,' Dobson said, making sheep's eyes at his intended.

Sherbourn glared. 'Not before I have a chance to speak with him.'

'I suggest you go in tandem,' Jasper said, irritated by their squabbles and, truth to tell, by all the loving glances.

'What a capital idea,' Patience said. 'Perhaps Mrs Durant will accompany you both.'

Amelia looked horrified. 'Certainly not. This is a thing best left to the gentlemen and your papa. I shall seek an appointment with him when I hear all has been settled to his satisfaction.'

'We certainly do not need a chaperon,' Sherbourn said.

At a dark glance from Jasper, he coloured. 'Not

that you haven't been most helpful, Mrs Durant, as I shall inform Mr Mitchell.'

She nodded graciously, but her demeanour didn't improve. Perhaps she was troubled by the fact that having failed to catch a duke for her heiress, her income would be less than she expected. Well, there was nothing he could do about that.

'Now that is settled,' he said, 'may I suggest we should all retire for an early night. It will be a long journey tomorrow and we had best be prepared for it.'

Quite honestly, he could not stand another moment of all this April-and-May stuff.

Everyone agreed with the suggestion and so he bade them goodnight.

After a sleepless night, Amelia knew that she had to speak to Jasper before she left Stone Hall. She had to apologise properly. If he refused to accept it, then there really was no more she could do, but she could not depart with the weight of her guilt hanging over her.

With the packing well under way, she went in search of Jasper.

Bedwell raise his eyebrows at her enquiry. 'I have not seen His Grace since he left for his morning ride.'

Oh, no. Had he gone out intending to return only after his guests had departed? She would not blame him if so. He must be disgusted with the lot of them.

She hurried to the stables. Riptide was in his stall.

'He returned an hour ago, miss,' a stable boy told her.

'Have you any idea where he went?'

He scratched at his ear and shook his head.

Next she tried his study. Not there. She ran up the winding staircase to his bedroom and nearly scared the maid making the bed out of her wits. 'I am looking for His Grace,' she said, not caring what the girl thought of her behaviour.

The girl pointed to the window. Amelia looked out and saw him sitting on a stone bench in a small walled garden she had not seen before.

'How do I get there?'

The maid shook out a pillow and placed it back on the bed. 'There is a door at the bottom of the stairs.'

She retraced her steps and found the small low wooden door leading out of the tower. Carefully she opened it and stepped outside. A heavenly mix of scents filled her nostrils. Lavender and rosemary and roses among them.

Jasper leaned forward, his chin resting in his palm, staring at a sprig of something he was twirling between finger and thumb. Not only was he alone, he looked dreadfully lonely.

Her courage gave way. He would not want her to see him this way.

She turned. The gravel crunched under her feet.

'Mrs Durant?'

Dash it. She turned back to him. 'Your Grace. I am sorry, I should not have disturbed you.'

He tossed the sprig aside. 'No matter. How may I be of assistance?' He smiled encouragingly, though his eyes were full of sadness.

Beneath his chilly exterior he was a good, kind

man. Pain pierced her heart. How could she have misjudged him so?

She swallowed. 'I wanted to apologise for believing all that awful stuff Albert said about you. It was unforgivable of me, but I want you to know how sorry I am.'

He gave her a cool smile. 'No matter. We all make mistakes.'

It did matter. But what more could she say if he cast off her apology so casually? 'I should go.'

'My mother planted this garden. The scents change with the season. I haven't been here for years, but this morning I felt in need of the memories it brings of her.'

'You miss her.'

'Foolish as it may seem, I do. Both of them. I was so angry when they died.' His chuckle sounded raw. 'I decided they could not possibly have loved me if they would risk their lives knowing I needed them. It helped me cope, being angry.'

Her heart ached for the boy who must have felt as if he'd been deserted. Her arms longed to offer comfort. But she did not have the right. 'Oh, Jasper, how dreadful for you. But you know they did not do it on purpose to hurt you.'

He sighed. 'I do, now. But it made my life dashed difficult, I must say. But I am holding you up. You are ready to depart, I presume? I told Bedwell to fetch me when the carriage was brought round.'

So Bedwell had known, but had been ordered

not to tell her. 'Thank you for your hospitality, Your Grace, and for your understanding.'

He bowed. 'You are welcome. And I imagine your reputation for making excellent matches remains unrivalled, even if you did not catch your heiress a duke.' There was a touch of bitterness in his tone.

She frowned. His words provoked a flash of insight. 'You already knew you would not make an offer for Charity when you invited us all to visit Stone Hall.'

His eyebrows shot up.

'You intended for her to fall into Lord Sherbourn's arms,' she continued, walking closer to him. 'Thereby saving her the embarrassment of not receiving an offer from you. You engineered the whole thing.' She saw it all now. Of course he would not have wanted Charity hurt after he decided not to make her an offer. That was who he was.

He shook his head. 'You are giving me too much credit, my dear. I had nothing to with Albert's schemes.'

'Of course not that part. You are far too kind and honourable to do anything of the sort. Oh, how I misjudged you on so many fronts.' Tears, hot and painful, welled up, making it hard to speak. 'How could you possible forgive me?' She turned away and scrabbled in her reticule for a handkerchief.

A large white folded square appeared over her shoulder and was pressed into her hand. 'My dearest Amelia. Please. I hate to think I am the cause of your upset. Do not cry.'

'But I am not your dearest Amelia,' she said, trying not to sob.

'Indeed you have been since the moment our eyes met at Sally Jersey's ball.'

Amelia looked up in shock as her gaze locked with his, hoping and yet disbelieving. 'Why did you not say so?'

'Because you were too busy trying to marry me off to an heiress for me to believe you cared for me in that way.'

The pain in her heart intensified. 'And then I went and let Albert convince me you were a terrible person. All this time, my heart has been telling me you are a good, kind man, but after my disastrous marriage, I could not trust my heart and I kept trying to keep you at bay. I was afraid. I am such a coward.' She sniffed.

He tipped her chin with a fingertip. 'Oh, my dear, not only are you beautiful, you are brave and courageous. And while your belief in Albert's accusations stung, you are not the only one to fall for his lies. I did so myself when I was a lad. Albert is clever.'

'Horrid man.' She dabbed at her eyes.

He sat down on the stone bench, smiling suddenly, as if his mind had cleared. Looking at Amelia with unmistakable fondness, he took her hand and pulled her on to his lap, then proceeded to use his handkerchief to dry her tears. 'My darling girl,' he murmured. 'Is it possible you can put aside your fears and give us a chance at happiness?'

'You still want to, after what I did?'

He smiled. 'Sweetheart, I do, with all my heart.

You are the only woman I have ever met who I could see standing at my side as my equal, my partner in both mind and heart.'

She sighed. 'Oh, Jasper.'

'I shall take that as a yes.'

He kissed her.

Epilogue

The double wedding at St George's Church of the Mitchell sisters that autumn would be spoken of by the *ton* in the same breathless tones that they had spoken of the marriages of the Gunnings in years past.

Seeing both girls so happy and both grooms as proud as punch, Amelia could not help but be pleased with her role in their matches.

'Are you satisfied?' Jasper asked as he stood behind her on the portico, watching them depart in brand new carriages emblazoned with coats of arms purchased by Papa Mitchell as wedding presents. A proud papa indeed.

'How could I not be?' Amelia said.

'Then we need make haste or we will miss a far more important wedding.'

'Far more important to whom?'

'To us, you wretched woman.'

Poor Jasper. She had made him promise to wait until after Charity and Patience's wedding She had not wanted to steal their thunder. Only Papa Mitchell knew that she and Jasper were to wed. She had felt it only right that she inform him of the circumstances and waive her fee from the settlements.

At first, he had been taken aback, but when he realised how happy his girls were with their choices of husbands and that he wasn't going to be out of pocket as far as Amelia was concerned, he had been exceedingly gracious.

Jasper took her arm and they slipped away, walking from Hanover Square to the ducal town house.

Aunt Mary met them at the door. 'Here you are at last. The Bishop is getting impatient.'

Jasper looked down his nose.

Amelia gave him a little dig in the ribs.

He grinned. 'You are ruining the ducal stare, my dear.'

Aunt Mary handed Amelia a bouquet of silk forget-me-nots, though she had been quite at a loss as to why Amelia had insisted on the flower. Amelia had requested them to tease Jasper because he still could not remember their first meeting.

They entered the drawing room together and found Lady Jersey entertaining the Bishop of London. The Bishop rose to his feet, clutching a glass of sherry. Jasper's valet and his butler stood at the side of the room, looking uncomfortable in their role as witnesses, but also terribly proud. Amelia smiled at them and they blushed.

'Your Grace,' Jasper said, bowing to the Bishop.

'Your Grace,' he replied.

Lady Jersey came forward and wagged a finger at Jasper. 'Sneaking up the back stairs again I see, Stone.'

He grinned. 'Amelia did not want a big fuss.'

'It is my second marriage,' Amelia said. 'I see no reason for us to make a spectacle of ourselves.'

'I still think we should have made a big splash,' Jasper said. 'I want everyone to know how happy I am.'

Lady Mary sighed. 'I am glad to hear you say it, Jasper. It is what I always wanted for you.'

Amelia believed her. Unfortunately, the dear lady had simply set about it the wrong way by making him suspect the motives of everyone around him, when he had already had doubts about his parents. Still, that was all in the past. She would make sure Jasper never had cause to doubt he was loved from now until for ever.

Lady Jersey turned to Amelia and gave her a hug. 'Well done, Mrs Durant. You will make a wonderful duchess. He needs someone to take him in hand and you are just the one.' She frowned at Jasper. 'I do wish you had let me know what you planned. I would have worn something a little more suited to the occasion.'

Jasper had said Sally was too much of a chatter-box to keep anything a secret, so he had merely sent round a note asking if she could call on him at eleven, as he had something important to discuss.

'You look divine as always,' Jasper said.

She giggled.

'Shall we begin?'

The butler whisked the Bishop's glass away. The Bishop stood in front of the hearth and Jasper took Amelia's hand.

The others in the room gathered behind them.

'Dearly beloved,' the Bishop said. 'We…'

Dearly beloved, Amelia thought. *That is exactly what I am.*

* * * * *